Shadow Lake

Shadow Lake

M. Jean Pike

Black Lyon Publishing, LLC

SHADOW LAKE
Copyright © 2009 by M. JEAN PIKE

Our books may be ordered through your local bookstore or by visiting the publisher:

www.BlackLyonPublishing.com

Black Lyon Publishing, LLC
PO Box 567
Baker City, OR 97814

This is a work of fiction. All of the characters, names, events, organizations and conversations in this novel are either the products of the author's vivid imagination or are used in a fictitious way for the purposes of this story.

ISBN-10:   1-934912-14-X
ISBN-13:   978-1-934912-14-0
Library of Congress Control Number: 2009922700

Written, published and printed in
the United States of America.

Black Lyon Contemporary Romance

For Elizabeth Parsons and Loretta Proctor,
my friends and fellow travelers on the road.
And for "Miss Deb," whose encouragement meant the world.

Chapter One

The scenery would have seemed glorious if she weren't having an anxiety attack.

Newly budded willows spread their branches like a canopy above the road, casting dappled shadows across Emma Beckman's path as her ancient Chevy navigated the precarious twists and turns. Where the trees thinned, a wall of cut rock hugged the hillside, blanketed with clusters of brilliant pink and lavender phlox. On another day, in another lifetime, Emma would have been enchanted, but not today.

Glancing at the directions she'd painstakingly copied from the Web site, she bit down on her lower lip. She should have found the place by now. A job out in the middle of nowhere, she thought. Strike one. Rounding another bend, she felt the engine stutter. And a beat-up old rust bucket to get there in. Strike two.

Reminding herself not to be negative, she turned on the radio and tried to concentrate on a morning talk show, but after a few moments waves of static overtook the perky voice of the female announcer and she turned it off.

She'd almost made up her mind to turn back when she saw a sign: *Shadow Lake Campground Two Miles Ahead*. Her nerves screamed in panic. A small part of her considered turning around anyway and heading back to town, forgetting the whole thing, but the biggest part knew that wasn't an option. This was the only job she'd come across in a month that she was even close to being qualified for. She had to go through with the interview no matter how much it jangled her nerves.

It won't be like the last time, she reassured herself, cringing at the memory of her short-lived career at the applesauce factory. She'd needed the money as desperately as she'd needed something to occupy her time and factory work seemed like a good fit. She could have gotten used to the noise, the stifling heat, and even the backbreaking work that sent her crashing into bed at night, every muscle in her body begging for mercy. But she knew before her first shift ended she would never adapt to her coworkers. She pretended not to notice the way the men stared at her, as if she was a new lunch selection in the vending machine, or the way the women ignored her timid attempts at conversation. By the end of the first week she gave up trying. Newly widowed and crushed by grief, she hadn't fit into their world of beer guzzling, bowling leagues and casual sex. They called her names behind her back: Miss Priss. Ice Queen. She could have dealt with that, but she could never handle their blatant sexual harassment.

She stuck it out for six months, kidding herself she was strong enough. And then one night it all came apart, and she knew she wasn't and never would be. She was working one of the faster lines that night, struggling to keep up as the jars of applesauce flew down the line at the alarming rate of five-hundred-fifty per minute. Jock Patterson, a notorious womanizer, was on the operating end. When she refused his offer to take her home at the end of their shift, he sped up the line, causing dozens of jars to crash to the floor and earning her a harsh reprimand from the team leader. She walked out in the middle of the shift feeling like an utter failure. Twenty-nine years old and she'd never had a real job. All she had was a useless Liberal Arts degree and a bunch of broken promises of happily-ever-after.

Oh, Beck, her heart cried. Honey, why didn't you think it through?

Tears welled in her eyes and she angrily blinked them back. She would not cry for Beck. Not today. Not ever again.

Rounding another bend, she saw a large, hand-carved sign: Welcome to Shadow Lake Campground! Easing into line behind a fifth-wheel camper, she nudged the Chevy into neutral and tried to calm her fluttering stomach.

After seeing the help wanted ad in the newspaper she'd pulled up the campground's Web site out of curiosity and saw that it boasted a quiet, shady retreat with lakefront cabins and sites for tents and motor homes. As beautiful as the Web site was, she saw that the photos hadn't done the campground justice. Tall pines, white birches and sugar maples flanked well worn paths that meandered down to a deep blue lake. Here and there, baskets of daffodils and grape hyacinth added splashes of gold and purple to the greenery.

When the entrance widened enough for her to pass, she skirted around the fifth-wheel and pulled into the first available slot. Turning off the engine, she took a moment to study the log cabin in front of her, a sign announcing Office posted prominently above the front door. A wide porch scattered with Adirondack chairs and wooden benches invited guests to sit and rest awhile. Beside the office was a rec hall, its open doors revealing ping-pong tables, arcade games and snack machines, and across from the rec hall was the quaint, log-built general store where she'd been instructed to report for an interview. On another day the building might have seemed intriguing. Today it loomed before her, threatening and unapproachable. Her hands trembled on the steering wheel as two thoughts collided in her head. I can't do this! I can't *not* do this!

As she sat there frozen with indecision, a teenaged boy wearing a baseball cap and a black T-shirt cruised past on a golf cart, the words *Shadow Lake Campground* stenciled on the side. He grinned, a small and meaningless gesture on his part, but it was so warm and genuine it somehow gave Emma courage. She hauled in a breath. Walk, Emma. Just put one foot in front of the other.

Glancing in the rearview mirror, she scrutinized her overgrown chestnut-colored hair and the dark circles that shadowed her eyes, despite the concealer she'd painstakingly applied that morning. Looking down, she considered her outfit, a knee-length denim skirt that had seen too many trips to the laundromat and a yellow camisole top and matching blouse she'd bought at the New-To-You Consignment Shoppe the day before. She'd been going for a capable, yet casual look, but now she feared she just looked shabby. There's no help for it, she thought, so you might as well make the best of it. On a last-minute impulse, she pulled her hair up into a clip, arranging a few stray tendrils in loose curls around her face. She took a swig of bottled water to moisten her parched throat, then got out of the car and headed toward the store.

•

"I'd like to check in now if it's not too much trouble."

Shane glanced up at the irritated summons, the second in three minutes' time. His stony gaze skimmed over the stout, red-faced man whose angry eyes glared back.

"I'll be right with you."

"That's what you said ten minutes ago," the man muttered.

Clenching his jaw, Shane turned his attention back to the impossible woman at the counter. She'd already chewed up fifteen minutes of his time dithering over disposable cameras and didn't seem to be an inch closer to making a decision.

"This one says it's best in bright light. It's awfully shady down on the paths."

"I'm sure either camera will do the job, Ma'am," he said, forcing all the diplomacy he could muster into his voice.

"I'm using it for birding and I need the photos to be clear. Now this one says high quality definition."

His jaw clenched again as she proceeded to read the entire package to him. Behind her, a frazzled mother scolded two dancing children who begged for fudgesicles. Two aisles over, an unruly toddler toppled a display of toothpaste. Good God, the store was in chaos.

The bell above the door chimed again and a pretty, young woman walked in. Shane took in the soft curve of her cheek, her large gray eyes, and the lustrous sheen of her hair, which perched in feminine disarray on top of her head. He didn't remember checking her into the campground, but then, the entire day had been a blur. His gaze traveled to the denim skirt that hugged her slim hips and the lemon-colored top that accentuated the soft swell of her breasts. He appreciated her beauty in the way an antique collector appreciates a finely-crafted piece of furniture — recognizing its loveliness but having no desire to own it. Because if he didn't know anything else on that early spring morning, Shane Lucy knew that he was through with women.

"I just don't know which one to buy," the camera lady whined. "What do you think I should ..."

A sharp yapping sound drew his attention to the back of the store. "Miss," he said sharply, interrupting the camera lady in mid-sentence, "you're going to have to take that dog out of here."

"I'm just going to grab a couple of things and then I'll get Sadie right out of your way," said a bleached blonde in a pair of red shorts and matching bikini top.

"No. Now!"

With a pop of her gum and a roll of her heavily made-up eyes, the girl pulled the yapping Corgi from the store. Returning his attention to the line of customers queued at the counter, he saw that the young mother had relented. Her children gleefully sucked on fudgesicles, leaving a dripping brown mess all over the floor.

"What do you have to do to get checked in around here?" the red- faced man bawled.

Shane ground his teeth together and cursed under his breath. *Thank you, Danielle*, he fumed. The girl had moved at the pace of a glacier but at least she'd known how to run a cash register. When he scolded her that morning for leaving the cash register unattended, and not for the first time, she walked out, leaving him in a damned mess. The campground wasn't even officially opened until Memorial Day, but hoping to take advantage of the unseasonably warm weather, Shane had opened a week early. He'd envisioned a slow but steady start to the season. He certainly hadn't expected to be left to single-handedly deal with this stampede.

That's what you get for hiring kids, he chided himself. But what choice did he have? There wasn't exactly a surplus of adults willing to work just five months out of the year. His most recent ad had only yielded one applicant over the age of twenty. He hoped to God this one would show up. His glance shot to the clock on the wall, and then to the woman in yellow who stood quietly off to the side and the realization dawned that he was looking at his newest employee.

"I just don't want to make the wrong decision, that's all," the camera lady said.

"Take them both," he said, shoving the cameras into the astonished woman's hands. "Bring back whichever one you don't use."

"Well that's a very sensible idea, young man. But here, they're both the same price so I'll pay you for one of them right now. That way I won't be beholden to you." He waited, his impatience flaring as she pulled out a change purse and counted five dollars' worth of coins into his hand. Catching the eye of the woman in yellow, he asked, "What can I do for you?"

"I'm l-looking for Shane L-lucy."

"You here about the job?"

She nodded, moistening her pretty, pink lips.

"Can you run a cash register?"

"Uh-huh."

When he motioned her behind the counter, he saw surprise register in her eyes, but she quickly complied.

"It's a standard PLU system, nothing complicated. Every item in the store is listed on this sheet," he said brusquely, tapping the sheet of paper that hung beside the register. "You just hit this button, key in the item number, and add the tax. This button right here. Got it?"

Her nervous glance darted from his eyes to the register. "I th-think so."

"Just do the best you can. I'll be right back." He abruptly walked from the store, motioning for the red-faced man to follow.

•

Emma barely had time to recover from her surprise. As a teenager she'd spent Saturday afternoons helping out in her aunt's South Street clothing boutique and was pretty sure the cash register had been a similar animal to the one she was looking at now. With trembling hands, she pushed her hair into place and went to work.

Her mistakes were many, but she made up for them with a bright smile as she engaged the customers in conversations about their vacation plans and most were happy to forgive her blunders. When the store was finally, mercifully empty, she got busy with a cloth and a bottle of spray cleaner and erased the trail of fudgy brown goo that stretched from the counter to the front door. She tidied a display of toiletries and swept discarded register receipts and footprints from the wide plank floor. In the back of the store, three small tables overflowed with litter. She threw out the Styrofoam cups and the dirty napkins and wiped the tables clean. With nothing left to do, she glanced out the window, wondering what had become of the angry, sexy man.

As if summoned by her thoughts, the door opened and he reappeared. Emma took stock of his dark hair and beard-stubbled chin, his unusual gold-flecked eyes. He was the ruggedly good looking kind of man that might model for a sportsman's magazine. Or a good anger management clinic, she thought with a chuckle.

His glance swept across the store. Seeing it was empty, he

pushed out a breath. "Maybe now we can talk for a minute."

He guided her to a table in the back of the store and slid into the seat across from her. His large, expressive eyes rested on her face. "I'm sorry; I can't remember your name."

"Emma B-beckman."

"Okay, Emma, like I told you on the phone, you'll be in charge of helping check in the campers and running the store. As you can see, it sometimes gets a little crazy in here."

She smiled. "I noticed."

"It's not usually quite so chaotic. I'm a little jammed up right now. I had a part-time girl but she quit without notice this morning, so I'll need help as soon as possible."

Hope swelled inside her. "Alright."

He gave her a rundown of the job description and the pay, the hours of work, and what her days off would be. "I guess that about covers it," he finally said. "Do you have any questions?"

"Why did the last girl quit?"

"She was a teenager," he said, as if that explained everything. When Emma continued to stare at him, he sighed. "She had a big attitude and an even bigger problem taking direction. She wasn't very motivated, unless it came to distracting my male workers." His glance skimmed over her. "I'm guessing that won't be a problem for you."

He might as well have reached across the table and slapped her, for as much as the comment stung. "I'm not in the habit of hitting on teenaged boys, if that's what you m-mean," she said, struggling to control her stutter.

"No, that's not what I meant."

Waves of anger and embarrassment washed over her and for a moment she was afraid she'd cry because she knew exactly what he'd meant. She wouldn't be a problem for his male workers because she was plain and unattractive. Her eyes ached with the effort of holding back tears.

Beck had thought she was lovely, and the beauty he saw in her had been his pride and joy. He was forever surprising her with jewelry, bottles of perfume, gift certificates to have her hair done at upscale salons. After Beck's accident the medical bills had chewed up their savings, and when he died, Emma had sold their house, a handyman special still in progress, for only a few thousand dollars more than was owed on it. Now she had to save what little money was left to pay the rent and keep the lights on in her shabby room on Fuller Street. There was no money for clothes, salons, or even a bottle of nail polish. But she was a hard and willing worker; she'd proved that today, hadn't she? And he'd not given her so much as a word of thanks or encouragement. All she had left was her battered pride, and she couldn't, wouldn't let this brute of a man take it from her.

"Could you could start tomorrow morning?" he asked, oblivious to her anger.

Gathering the shreds of her dignity, she stood. "I d-don't think I'm interested in the j-job after all. But thank you for your time."

He reached out his hand as if he meant to touch her, but seeing her angry expression, let it fall back to his side. "Look, about what I said, it came out wrong. I didn't mean--"

The bell above the front door chimed and a voice boomed out, "Hello? Is this where we're supposed to check in?"

He passed a hand over his face and pushed out a breath. "Just wait here, alright?"

While he trudged up front to deal with the customer, Emma quietly slipped out the back door.

Chapter Two

A job in the middle of nowhere. *A beat-up old rust bucket to get there in, and an arrogant ass for a boss,* Emma thought, jamming her key into the ignition. *Strike three. You're out.*

Pulling from the lot, she gave in to the tears that had threatened since morning. As she navigated down the winding road she'd climbed so hopefully only an hour before, she felt her anger turn to despair. *Congratulations, Emma. You just lost the only job in a month you were halfway qualified for. Now what?*

Trying to calm down and think rationally, she ran through her list of options. Waitressing? She was pretty sure she needed experience to get into one of the city's upscale restaurants and make any kind of decent money. With what she knew about waiting tables the best she could hope for was a night shift at one of the rundown diners in the bar district along the river. Sales? She'd already applied at every retail store in town. Receptionist? She winced, thinking of the five hours she'd put in as a temp in a busy pediatrician's office. Trying to transfer the nonstop phone calls that came through, she'd inadvertently disconnected more callers than she'd put through and the disgruntled doctor had called the agency before the day's end demanding a replacement.

The woman at the agency had been kind, but firm, saying that perhaps Emma needed to give herself more time, that perhaps it was too soon. And it was too soon. After a year, the pain of losing Beck was still too raw, too jagged. But the electric company didn't care about her mental state of affairs and neither did her landlord. She was left with only one option, and she couldn't bear the thought of it.

"You'll have to come home now, I suppose."

Her mother's voice echoed like the memory of an unpleasant

dream inside her head. Miranda made the thin-lipped, grudging offer at Beck's funeral and Emma had politely turned it down. To run back to Philly and live under her parents' roof at almost thirty years of age, to slip back into the role she'd been so desperate to break free of? No, that felt too much like failure.

Emma had often wondered what her appearance-conscious mother and workaholic father expected when they adopted her as a small child. Certainly not the awkward adolescent she'd grown into. She knew even then she wasn't the child Miranda Bayleigh dreamed of, that she was a disappointment. Every beauty pageant she didn't win and every birthday party invitation she didn't receive was just another concrete slab in the wall between her and her disillusioned mother. Add to that a speech impediment even the top speech pathologists in the city couldn't cure and what you had was a bona fide dysfunctional childhood.

Seeing that even the child she'd been so desperate for was not enough to make his wife happy, Emma's father retreated farther into his work, leaving Emma to bear the brunt of Miranda's displeasure alone. When Emma finally blossomed, at age sixteen, Miranda saw it as a second chance to force her daughter into the mold she'd so stubbornly cast for her. She chauffeured her to dance lessons, cheerleading practices and Honor Society meetings. She chose the girls Emma was allowed to hang out with and hand-picked the boys she was allowed to date, rejecting the very ones Emma felt the most comfortable with. She grew up in the shadow of Miranda's displeasure, stripped of self-confidence, having every advantage a child could want, and none of the love a child craves. Her entire existence changed the day she met Tim Beckman.

She was in her freshman year of college, a Liberal Arts major, and Beck was a grounds and maintenance worker. With his easy smile and his absolute acceptance of who she was, Emma fell madly, irrevocably in love. In her senior year, Beck was offered a job at a construction company in upstate New York and they eloped the day after her college graduation, leaving Philadelphia and Miranda's iron-fisted rule behind forever. Or so she thought.

Oh, Beck ... Why didn't you think it through?

Her tears fell hard and fast and she scanned the shoulder of the road in search of a place wide enough to pull over and compose herself. Drifting to the side, she heard a loud popping sound seconds before a rolling cloud of steam drifted out from under the hood of her car.

"Oh, no!" she wailed, beating the steering wheel with her fist.

Climbing out of the car, her first impulse was to open the hood, but what good would that do? Even if she could figure out the problem, she hadn't the first clue what to do about it. As she stood gazing at the sputtering car her second impulse was to walk back to the campground. Thinking of the smug smile that would probably be on Shane Lucy' face, her third was to lie down on the side of the road and die. Just die.

Oh for God's sakes, Emma, don't be such a drama queen, she scolded herself. Gathering her determination, she turned and marched back toward the campground.

She hadn't taken more than a few steps when she heard a low rumbling sound and turned to see the boy on the red golf cart coming up the road behind her. She continued walking until he caught up and idled beside her.

"Looks like you've got a problem with your radiator." He'd removed his baseball cap and Emma's eyes skimmed over his green Mohawk, crisply gelled into half inch Liberty spikes, and the silver hoop that glinted from his lip.

"Looks like," she said.

"Hop in. I'll give you a ride back to the campground."

She gratefully climbed in beside him. "Thank you."

"No problem."

"I'm glad you came along when you d-did. Two miles up this road in these babies, my feet would have been begging for m-mercy," she said, indicating her black, chunky heeled sandals.

"I had to go down and weed eat around the signs, otherwise I'd be cleaning the bathrooms right now," he said, adding with a grin, "And you'd be S.O.L."

She grinned back.

"My name's Mick, by the way."

"Emma."

"I saw you at the campground earlier. Are you going to be working there?"

"N-no, probably not."

He nodded.

She regarded him with curiosity. "How do you like working

there?"

He shrugged. "I'm sixteen. Where else am I gonna work?"

"Your boss, Mr. Lucy - he seems a little bit abrupt."

Mick snorted. "Ya think?"

She chuckled, feeling an instant kinship with the boy. When they rounded the last bend and the campground came into view, he jammed the baseball cap on his head, neatly covering his spikes. "I'm not allowed to show my hair," he explained. "He says it will make the campers nervous."

She chuckled again, but her amusement quickly turned to apprehension when they pulled up in front of the general store.

"Here you are," Mick said. "Safe and sound."

"Thanks M-mick. I appreciate it." Without quite thinking, she added, "You're a good kid."

Something flickered in his eyes, something vague and longing she couldn't quite name. Before she could analyze it, it was swallowed up by a grin as he waved and drove away.

•

Shane hadn't expected to see her again, and certainly not within an hour of her departure. He'd known the moment the comment came out of his mouth that he'd said something stupid, that he'd somehow wounded her. He regretted it, even though he wasn't exactly sure what he'd said that was so wrong. When had he become such an insensitive ass?

He tried to brush the morning's episode off, telling himself he didn't have time to sit around analyzing women, and that if Emma Beckman was going to go to pieces every time he spoke a harsh word, then the campground was better off without her.

Now she stood before him, flushed and pretty and his sensibilities stirred again. He wondered what had brought her back, but before his mind could form the question, she asked one of her own.

"Do you m-mind if I use your phone?"

With a flip of the hand, he indicated the pay phone in the back of the store.

"I d-don't suppose you'd happen to know of a good wr-wrecker service?"

Ahhhhh. "Car trouble?"

"Radiator."

He folded his arms across his chest. "Maybe I could look at it for you."

Hope flickered in her eyes, but she stubbornly tilted her chin. "No, thank you."

"A tow back to the city's going to cost a fortune."

She nodded. "Probably."

"I'm guessing a hundred bucks."

Panic registered in her eyes but she remained silent.

"Like I said, maybe I could look at it for you."

"You know about c-cars?"

He laughed. "Honey, I run a business with a bunch of old dinosaurs I can't begin to afford to replace. Let's just say I know my way around underneath a hood."

She stared at him, weighing his offer, obviously at war with herself.

"I'll make you a deal," he said. "I'll look at your car if you'll give me another shot at an interview. Clean slate."

She pushed out a reluctant breath. "Alright."

He thrust out his hand. "I'm Shane Lucy. Have we met?"

Despite herself, she grinned and he noticed two perfect dimples appear at the sides of her mouth. "Emma Beckman."

"Thank you for coming in today, Emma. If you wouldn't mind watching the store for a moment, I have a radiator to see to."

"My pleasure."

He retrieved a two-way radio from his belt and pressed the call button. "Mick, grab the truck and the tow dolly and meet me at the store."

"Ten-four," came Mick's static-filled reply.

Moments later a pickup truck pulled up out front and Shane left the store, grumbling inside his head about the loss of an entire afternoon's work. He told himself that in the long run he was doing himself a favor. If ever the campground needed another set of hands, it was now. He told himself helping Emma Beckman out was purely good business sense, and he told himself it had nothing to do with her tantalizing figure or her beautiful gray eyes.

Chapter Three

The afternoon at the store went much more smoothly than the morning, with only the occasional customer popping in for a bundle of kindling wood or a bottle of ketchup. Emma was glad nothing pressing came up, since Shane had driven into the city to see about parts for her car. Having gotten over the first hurdle, the last thing she wanted was to start her new job with a show of incompetence, with more broken jars of applesauce.

Alone in the store, she took the opportunity to familiarize herself with the inventory. The store sold all of a vacationer's basic needs: shampoo and toothpaste, condiments and lighter fluid, even a selection of paddle balls and coloring books for antsy children on unexpected rainy days. The freezer was stocked with ice cream sandwiches, popsicles, and nutty bars, with a large cooler in the back for beer and soda. Emma made a mental note to ask Shane about adding bottled water, and possibly a small selection of fresh fruits, like grapes and watermelon, and maybe a few quarts of fresh strawberries.

At the end of the day she paper clipped the sales receipts together and put them in the bank bag beneath the counter, along with the money from the register. She tidied up disheveled displays, prepared the coffee pots for the next morning, swept the floor, and emptied the wastebaskets. Remembering she'd seen a dumpster outside the back door earlier that day, she gathered up the garbage bags and slipped outside.

The sound of angry voices greeted her, and her gaze traveled across the alley to where Shane and Mick were working on her car.

"I've said all I'm going to say on the subject, Mick. You don't need to be worrying about this crap right now."

"Like you know what I need," Mick retorted.

Shane slammed the hood down on the car. "I said I'm done talking about it."

Emma cringed at the harshness in his voice, wondering how he kept any workers at all. She stood there, holding the garbage bag, until both of them turned and looked in her direction.

"Is it five o'clock already?" Shane asked.

She cleared her throat. "Nearly quarter past."

"How did it go?"

"Pretty well, I think."

"Why don't you go ahead and lock up the store then. Mick, you can take Emma around and show her the campground."

Mick nodded and walked away, his face still flushed with anger. She'd just turned the sign to closed and locked the front door when he pulled up in the golf cart. "Hop in," he said, the anger seething in his eyes belying his easy smile.

He navigated down a wide path flanked on either side by rows of large campers, most of them equipped with small flower gardens and built-in decks. "These are the permanents," Mick explained. "They rent these spots every year for the whole summer. You don't really need to worry too much about them."

A woman sat on her deck, reading a book. She smiled and waved as they passed by. "Evening, Mick," she called.

"Hey, Mrs. Conroy."

When they were out of earshot, Mick said, "Most of the permanents are pretty easy to get along with. It's the weekend warriors that are a pain in the butt." He turned off on a side path, where several deep, shady lots were dotted with pop up campers and small motor homes. "These sites are rented by the day," he explained. "They all come with electric hookups, in case anyone asks, and most of them are pull-throughs."

"Pull-throughs?"

"Sites where the campers can be pulled in straight on, instead of backed in. For what they pay for these things, most of these rich old farts don't have a clue how to drive them." He grinned and Emma sensed his earlier tension evaporating.

Her glance swept across the woods, where a pair of chipmunks zigzagged up the side of a poplar in hot pursuit of one another, while a chorus of birds trilled their evening concerto. The atmosphere was soothing, almost hypnotic, and she was glad she'd changed her mind.

After the morning's debacle, Shane had worked hard to make things right with her, even saying she could pay back the cost of the car repairs a little each week. Knowing she was indebted to him was unsettling. Like it or not, now she was obligated to stay, at least for the summer. She considered the bright blue sky and the sparkling lake in the distance. There were definitely worse places to be stuck.

Mick swung wide down another trail and pointed out a dozen no-frills plots which he identified as tent sites, and then moved on to the final leg of the tour. They rumbled down a gentle incline and came upon a cluster of white wood-framed cottages, their trim painted a bright, cheerful red. Each came equipped with a grill, a picnic table, and a pair of old fashioned metal rocking chairs painted glossy greens and blues.

The deep, throaty bass of heavy metal music abruptly shattered the quiet and Mick switched off the golf cart and fished a cell phone from his baggy pocket. "Yeah? Oh, hey."

His tone softened, telling Emma the caller was female. He lowered his voice and turned away. "I'm not going to be able to go." After a pause, he said, "Because my dad's being a jackass, that's why."

Emma thought of the heated exchange she'd witnessed and the realization that Shane was Mick's father dawned with the subtlety of a hurricane. Why hadn't she guessed? Mick's coloring was much lighter, and his eyes, a dusty blue rather than the gold-flecked hazel of his father's, but scrutinizing his profile, she saw the same square jaw line, the same full lower lip.

"I know, baby. I know."

Feeling like an auditory Peeping Tom, Emma climbed out of the golf cart and wandered down to the lakefront, her mind still chewing on this new piece of information. She hadn't thought her boss much more than thirty, but if Mick was sixteen, then Shane had to be much older than she'd guessed. That, or he'd gotten an extremely early start on fatherhood. He didn't wear a wedding ring and she'd assumed he was single. The thought that he had a wife and son was jarring somehow, though she couldn't imagine why. Shane could be charming, but he could also be harsh, she'd seen that for herself. He was phenomenally good-looking, sure, but she hadn't been affected by another man's looks since the day she met Beck. Shane Lucy didn't mean a thing to her, so what was this curious disappointment swirling around inside of her?

"Sorry about that." Mick's voice broke in on her thoughts and she turned to see him watching her. "I think I've pretty much showed you everything. Are you ready to head back?"

She climbed back up the embankment and seated herself in the golf cart beside him. Knowing she should leave it alone, but not quite able to, she asked, "Shane's your dad?"

He started up the cart and drove back toward the store. "Yup."

They rode in silence for a while.

"He didn't used to be such a hard ass. He's been like this ever since my mother left."

Emma felt her insides shift again. "Your mother left you?"

"She took off about a year ago. We haven't seen her since."

"I'm sorry, Mick."

He shrugged. "I'm not." But the earlier emotion flickered in his eyes again, telling Emma differently.

•

Shane turned his wrench on the last bolt, snugged it tight, and slammed the hood with a sense of satisfaction. That should hold it. For now, anyway. He considered the car, a late nineties Chevy with all the wear and tear of a car twice its age. While he was under the hood he'd taken the time to replace a couple worn belts as well as the radiator, but the car needed more help than he could offer. He'd give it another five thousand miles, at the most.

His thoughts returned to Emma and he wondered what her deal was. The fact that she'd allowed him to fix her car even though she was plainly still angry with him told him she didn't have a man of her own to rely on. A cute girl like her, he couldn't help wondering why. A second thought occurred to him, and his expression soured.

"They're all cute until you get them in front of a judge," he muttered.

Thoughts of Blair invaded like a kick in the gut, and he wondered how he could still feel so much anger, so much pain. Seventeen years together, and in the end it had added up to nothing.

They'd married young, barely eighteen-years-old, but he'd always thought of that as a good thing. He'd foolishly thought that having history together would give their relationship staying power. It was hard, those early years, raising a baby under his parents' roof. They couldn't seem to stop instructing him and Blair on everything from parenting to finances, couldn't seem to stop seeing them as kids. When they retired to Florida and sold Shane the campground, he thought things would get easier. He and Blair could be on their own, make their own decisions and raise their son without interference.

While owning their own home and business had been liberating, it had also brought responsibilities Shane hadn't bargained for. Blair accused him of being distant, a workaholic, even went so far as to say she'd outgrown him. But maybe those were all just excuses for the real truth. She was tired of him. Tired of the life they'd spent nearly two decades struggling to build. So she'd gone her own way. Gone off to experience life, which Shane took to mean experience other men.

He felt the knife twist in his gut again. Blair was the only lover he'd ever had. Her love had been enough for him, though obviously his hadn't been enough for her.

In the end she'd taken half of his assets and all of his faith in marriage and commitment and left him with a struggling business and a teenaged son she didn't want to parent and he didn't know how to.

His thoughts swung to his latest altercation with Mick and he sighed. If he'd known that Mick and Danielle had a thing going, he wouldn't have hired her in the first place. She was eighteen. Two full years, and Shane suspected an entire universe more experienced than Mick. When he caught them making out in the storage shed he'd been livid, determined to find a way to make the girl quit without actually firing her and incurring his son's wrath. God, he didn't want to be the bad guy again. It wasn't that he didn't understand how it was to be sixteen and so hung up on a girl you couldn't think straight, of course he did. He just didn't want to see Mick walk the same hard road he had.

Hearing the rumble of the golf cart, he grabbed a clean rag and wiped his hands, then wiped a smudge of grease from Emma's fender. Moments later she stood before him, looking lovely with the afternoon sun in her hair.

"You're all set," he said, handing her the car keys.

"Thank you."

"You should really think about trading this in."

"I'll give it some th-thought." She handed him the bank bag from the store. "I wasn't sure what to do with this."

As he reached for the bag, his hand brushed against hers, sending a burning sensation slamming through his veins. "You did a good job today," he said.

She blushed. "Thanks."

"Listen, I know we got off to a rough start, and I apologize."

She waved the words away as she opened her driver's side door and climbed in. "Like you said, c-clean slate."

He'd thawed a package of hamburger that morning, and it was on the tip of his tongue to invite her to stay for a cookout, but she was already starting the car, already putting it into gear.

"I'll see you in the morning, then?" he said instead.

She smiled. "You bet."

He watched as she pulled from the lot, his body still reacting to her touch. He'd gone almost a year without the touch of a woman's hands. As she rounded the corner and disappeared, he trudged back toward the house, his heart trying to convince his body he was better off.

Chapter Four

The next morning Emma awoke before the alarm went off, feeling lighter than she had in weeks. She lay in bed for a moment, savoring the knowledge that she had a job—one she was confident she could handle. Images of Shane Lucy flitted into her mind and she pushed them away, telling herself her new boss had nothing to do with her positive new outlook on life.

She treated herself to a honeysuckle-scented bath and dressed in a black, ankle-length skirt and her favorite emerald green top, then dried her hair and arranged it in soft waves around her shoulders before padding to the kitchen for breakfast. She lingered over a second cup of coffee, and then, humming a small tune, she got in her car and headed for Shadow Lake.

Climbing the winding road, she noticed fields of early wildflowers where the forest thinned, and an occasional cabin tucked into the hillside. She drank in the beauty of the landscape, wondering how she'd happened to miss it the day before.

At 7:45 she pulled into the campground parking lot, turned off the engine, and headed for the office, slowing her footsteps when she heard heated words drifting through the open window.

"If you're not mature enough to be in school, then you're not mature enough to take my truck to the city. End of discussion."

"Fine! Just forget I asked."

Before she could knock, the door opened and Mick's angry eyes stared into hers. "Hey, Emma," he said, dropping his gaze as he stormed past. She hesitated for a moment, waiting for Shane to appear. When he didn't, she stepped inside the office.

The room was small and cozy, constructed of knotty pine paneling and large, sunny windows. A glance to her right revealed a waiting area where a settee and a pair of easy chairs sat beside a coffee table scattered with stacks of colorful pamphlets. To her left were a pair of file cabinets and a desk holding a computer, a telephone, and a fax machine. Behind the office area a door stood open. Emma crept toward it, venturing a soft, "Hello?"

She heard footsteps and then Shane appeared before her, bare-chested and dressed in a pair of well worn jeans, his hair damp and disheveled. Her breath caught and she felt her face grow warm.

"Hey, I wasn't expecting you quite so early," he said. "Come on in."

She stepped through the doorway and into a space that oozed masculinity. She took in the sturdy leather furniture and the tastefully framed wildlife prints that were clustered in mismatched groups on the honey pine walls. Wrought iron anchors and stunningly lifelike wooden decoys adorned the coffee and end tables, while bold throw rugs in deep burgundies and greens were scattered about the wide plank floor. Though far from spotless, the room had a quality of lived-in orderliness that Emma found appealing.

She followed Shane through to the kitchen, where a farmer's table was littered with breakfast dishes. Shane scooped them up and dumped them in the sink. "Coffee?"

"Please."

He poured her a man-sized cup before setting a sugar bowl and a carton of Half and Half on the table in front of her. She dumped a teaspoonful of sugar into her cup and stirred, looking everywhere except at his bare chest.

"I thought I'd show you the ropes in the office this morning, if that's alright," he said.

"That's fine."

"Great. I'm going to go and finish getting dressed and then we'll get started."

"Great," she echoed, unable to keep from staring at his broad back and heavily muscled arms as he disappeared down the hallway.

Fifteen minutes later she was back in the office. "The office pretty much takes care of itself. I check the answering machine a few times a day and return any important calls. People who want to check in will come directly to the store."

He showed her the appointment book and the schedule of rates, then booted up the computer. "Have a seat," he said, indicating the swivel chair beside his. She obediently sat down, watching as he keyed in the password, Blair. The computer whirred and clicked, and finally complied. Shane pulled up the registry and showed her how to log in reservations. Emma did her best to concentrate, but his nearness was unsettling. Beck had always preferred a citrus-scented after shave. Shane's was deep and woodsy, fitting for a man of the great outdoors. An image of his wide shoulders and well toned biceps popped into her head and she felt a tingling sensation in her nether regions.

"I think that about covers it," he said, after he'd patiently explained the process. "Have you got any questions?"

"It seems pretty cut and dried," she said.

"We set it up as simply as possible when we took over. Sort of like, Running a Campground for Dummies." He grinned, showing off a set of perfect, white teeth.

You and Blair? She thought, wondering at the small pinprick of jealousy she felt.

"The store doesn't open until ten, so you can hang out in here until then. I've got a water leak down in area four. I'll probably be there for most of the morning, but Mick will be around." He opened a drawer, removed a two-way radio, and handed it to her. "Just holler if you need anything."

•

The next two hours passed uneventfully. Emma took three calls from people reserving tent sites for the following weekend and managed to enter the credit card information without crashing the computer. At ten o'clock she opened the general store and set the coffee pots to perking. At a few minutes past, some of the permanents wandered in, filling Styrofoam cups as they perused the morning paper at the small tables near the back. Most were friendly and welcoming, and Emma guessed they'd stopped by as much to check out the new girl on the block as for their morning fuel-up. She chatted them up about their hobbies and looked at their photos of children and grandchildren, and by the morning's end most of them seemed like old friends.

At noon Mick poked his head in the door.

"My dad told me to come and kick you out of here."

She grasped the edge of the counter. "Why?"

He grinned. "It's lunch time. I'm supposed to spot you for a half hour, so get going."

Relief pooled in her belly and she returned his grin. "Oh."

He ambled to the cooler and grabbed a bottle of soda, downing it in one large, thirsty gulp. "We've got some killer microwavable hoagies here if you're interested," he said, removing a red-and-white striped package.

"I brought my lunch today, but I'll sure keep that in mind for n-next time."

She went to her car and retrieved the brown bagged lunch of tuna salad and bottled water she'd packed the night before, then headed back to the porch, where Mick was sprawled out on a glider, munching on his sub. "You can go and eat by the lake if you want to," he said around a mouthful of meatballs.

"I think I'd rather stay here, if that's alright."

"Suit yourself," he said, sliding over to make room for her.

She sat down beside him, opened her water, and took a swallow.

"How do you like working here?" Mick asked.

"So far, so good."

"That's cool."

"You seem like your f-father's right-hand man."

He snorted. "I'm his slave is more like it. He's working me like a dog this week."

"I imagine there's a lot to do with opening weekend coming up."

"It's not that." He swallowed the last bite of his sandwich and chased it down with a swig of soda. "He's punishing me."

"Punishing you for what?"

"I got suspended from school again."

"Oh."

"I got in a fist fight," he volunteered. "And I'd do it again if I had to."

Emma regarded him thoughtfully. "You don't seem like the f-fighting kind."

He shrugged. "I am when I have to be."

Not sure how to respond, Emma sipped her water. A cool breeze whispered across the lot, playing with her hair and fluttering the leaves of a nearby maple tree. Searching for a conversation piece,

Emma asked, "Do you play any sports, Mick?"

"Nah. I would have liked to have tried out for soccer, but my grades aren't too great this year."

"What do you like to do in your spare time?"

"Skateboard, hang out with my friends. Unproductive stuff like that." He grinned and she knew the last words were Shane's.

Before she could comment, the pickup truck pulled up to the store and Shane rolled down the window. "I see you got your lunch okay."

She raised her bottle of water in a toast.

"I have to run into town and pick up some parts for the pump." He directed his gaze to Mick. "Want to ride along?"

"Nah. I've got too much stuff to do." Mick stood, jammed his hands in his pockets, and slunk away.

Watching him go, Shane sighed. "I guess he's still mad at me."

Emma played with her water bottle, not sure what, if anything, to say.

"I wish kids came with a manual. I could sure use the Raising Teenagers for Dummies edition."

"It's hard," Emma said.

"Do you have kids?"

"No, but it looks hard."

"And it's even harder than it looks." He chuckled, but his expression was grim. "Guess I'll head in to town, then, if he's going to mope." His gaze rested on her for a long moment. "Would you like to stay after work and have dinner with us?"

It was the last thing Emma expected him to say, and she was momentarily struck dumb. "I'd l-like that," she said, regaining her sensibilities.

"Good, then. I'll see you this evening, if not before." He rolled up his window and drove away, leaving Emma to stare after him.

She thought about the conversation for the rest of the afternoon. Like a sudden cloudburst on a sunny day, the invitation had come completely out of the blue, sending her scrambling for some sort of umbrella by which to explain it.

They were talking about Mick and Shane's feelings of inadequacy as a parent. Maybe he simply wanted another presence at the table, someone to act as a buffer between himself and his son's anger. But something in his eyes hinted there was more to it than that.

At five o'clock she locked up the store and ducked into the bathroom to brush her hair and apply a coat of lipstick before heading across the parking lot. Letting herself in through the office door, she heard the sound of raucous music playing and followed it to the kitchen, where Mick stood at the counter shredding a brick of cheddar cheese.

He glanced up when she entered. "I hope you like tacos," he said, reaching to lower the volume on the radio.

"I love tacos. What can I do to help?"

"I thought you'd never ask," he said with a grin. He set her up with a head of lettuce, a large ripe tomato, and a knife, then went back to work on the cheese. He chatted about the new Adam Sandler movie he wanted to see, his conversation ending abruptly when Shane appeared in the doorway.

"You've put our guest to work?" His tone was light, but his disapproving glance lingered on his son's face.

"I offered," Emma interjected. Her eyes sought his with what she hoped was a subtle message. Lighten up, okay?

Moving to the stove, she crumbled a package of ground beef into a fry pan, gently stirring as it began to sizzle. Shane looked over her shoulder into the pan. His woodsy scent filled her senses and she felt her stomach flutter. As a teenager she'd had a crush on a football player named Tommy Addison. She was so dumbstruck by his good looks that she couldn't even seem to talk when he was in the same room. She hadn't thought of Tommy in years, and realized with no small amount of surprise that she was reacting in the exact same way to her new boss. Mercifully, he moved to the cupboard, removed a stack of plates, and began to set the table.

Their dinner conversation was polite, if strained. Still, Emma couldn't help thinking how nice it was to sit down to a meal she didn't have to eat alone. She asked a hundred and one questions about the campground, and answered as many about what it was like growing up in Philadelphia, babbling non-stop about the horticultural gardens in Fairmount Park, the Museum of Art, and the Phillies in an attempt to fill the stony silence between her two companions. More than once she found her gaze traveling across the table to Shane, insufferably sexy with a dash of salsa on his chin. The meal over, she was searching her mind for another conversation starter when a loud knock at the door interrupted the quiet.

"It's open," Shane called.

A man Emma recognized as one of the permanent campers poked his head in. "Hey, I'm sorry to bother you, Shane, but my electric hookup doesn't seem to be working."

"Mrs. Hogan probably popped a breaker again. I'll go take a look." He shoved back his chair and stood, telling Emma, "I'll be right back."

Mick stood and began to clear the plates from the table.

"It must be hard living with the constant interruptions," Emma said, remembering well the countless interrupted dinners and the nights out that had been postponed whenever Beck received an unexpected service call.

Mick rinsed the dishes and stacked them in the dishwasher. "You get used to it."

She gathered up the leftover salsa and sour cream, scraped them back in their containers, and stowed them in the fridge. She thought of the heated exchange she'd overheard that morning. Having learned the hard way that life was too short to fill with negative emotions, she felt compelled to try and help repair the damage. Unsure how to go about it, she ventured, "I think your dad's feeling bad about the argument you two had this morning."

"Then maybe he should stop treating me like I'm ten years old," Mick said, jamming a fry pan in the dishwasher.

"He's doing the best he can, Mick," she said gently.

"I don't care. I hate him."

"You don't mean that."

"He doesn't even try to understand where I'm coming from. I mean, if some dude would have called my mom a slut he'd have kicked their ass, no questions asked. But I'm supposed to walk away and be a bigger man. That's bull."

"I can see why that would make you want to p-punch somebody's lights out," she said, "Saying nasty things like that about your mom."

He let loose a short, sharp bark of laughter. "I wouldn't have cared about that. My mom is a slut. They said it about my girlfriend."

His inner turmoil was palpable. At that moment he was sixteen, going on four. He was a mixed bag of anguish and testosterone and insecurity she didn't begin to know how to soothe, but still, she felt the need to try.

"I think your dad's just trying to look out for you."

"No he's not. He's punishing me."

"For what, Mick?"

He shrugged and slammed the dishwasher shut. Grabbing a cloth, he scrubbed at the countertops and then the table. When he'd wiped them clean, he tossed the dishcloth in the general direction of the sink and turned away from her, hands jammed in his pockets. Emma was thinking she'd done enough damage for the night and that it was probably best if she left. She was about to say as much when Mick delivered the second unexpected rainstorm of the day.

"I don't know how long he's gonna be gone. You wanna play Yahtzee or something?"

With no available umbrella, and nothing else to do but see it through, she smiled. "Sure."

•

Returning home, Shane was surprised to hear laughter coming through the open windows. Curious, he stepped around to the side of the house and peeked in. Mick and Emma sat at the table, playing Yahtzee, of all things. Emma with her pretty, pink mouth, the soft overhead light doing amazing things to her hair. She playfully wagged a finger at Mick, scolding him with a smile that could light up the universe. Mick gave it back to her, completely unabashed, completely Mick. They seemed as comfortable together as if they were old pals and Shane felt a pang. Why couldn't he seem to get to that place of easy friendship with his son?

Heading inside, he stood in the doorway, enjoying their banter until Emma glanced up and noticed him there.

"What's going on in here?" he asked.

Surprisingly, it was Mick who answered. "Not much. Just that Miss Emma's getting her butt kicked."

"Yeah, well n-next time I'm bringing my own dice because these are definitely loaded," she shot back, showing off her killer set of dimples. "Wanna play?"

"If he's playing, I'm not," Mick said, but without malice.

Shane grinned. "Aww, come on. Why would you say such a thing?"

"Of course he can play," Emma said, swatting Mick's arm. "The more the merrier."

"That's what you say now. What you don't know is that my dad is a very sore loser."

"And you know this how?" Shane said, ambling toward the table. "I can't recall that I've ever lost a game."

Mick rolled his eyes with an exaggerated sigh. "Oh, here we go."

Shane slid into a chair and indicated the stack of blank score sheets.

"Set me up, Miss Emma."

●

It was the most enjoyable evening she'd spent in months, despite the fact she'd lost all twelve rounds of the game. Emma was having such a good time she didn't notice the moments turning into hours until she looked at the clock.

"Gosh, I should get going. It's almost t-ten o'clock."

"Do you want to stay?" Shane asked. "You could sleep in the guest room."

The invitation was innocent enough on the surface, but something subtle in his eyes and in his tone of voice hinted at danger. Or maybe she was just imagining things. Maybe she was just so lonely …

"N-no, I should go home."

He walked her to her car and waited while she dug out her keys.

"I can't remember when I've enjoyed an evening more, Emma. Thanks for staying."

"Thanks for inviting me."

Time seemed to slow and then stop completely and Emma got the scared, dizzy sensation the moment was going to end in a kiss. She turned abruptly and opened the car door. "S-see you in the morning, Shane."

"Watch out for deer, Miss Emma," he said softly.

Driving home, her head was reeling but her heart was strangely content. She spent a few moments in analyzing the warm and wonderful feeling coursing through her body and realized with surprise that it was happiness. She couldn't remember feeling truly unburdened, truly happy since before Beck's accident.

The feeling evaporated the moment she walked in her front door.

Chapter Five

Emma froze, a fist of apprehension clenching in her stomach. From the end of the dimly lit hallway she could see the door to her apartment was ajar. She'd left in a hurry that morning, but there was no way she would have taken off without locking her door. Catching her breath, she crept closer.

The door knob hung crookedly in its slot, dented beyond recognition, as if it had been smashed with a maul. She crouched to study the damage, lightly running her fingers over the remains. Someone had definitely forced their way inside her apartment. Steeling herself against the inevitable, she nudged the door open.

"Oh, n-no," she bleated. Her gaze skimmed across the room, taking in the overturned stereo, the CDs scattered across the floor and the wreckage that only that morning had been her television set. Her glance darted to the empty space on her desk where her laptop should have been and wasn't, and she fought the urge to cry.

Through the open bathroom door she could see her towels and nightclothes strewn about on the floor. In the kitchen, the contents of her refrigerator had been dumped in messy piles on the cracked linoleum. She slumped against the wall, surveying the damage. It looked as though a tornado had swept through. A very angry tornado, at that. She searched her memory for possible enemies, for people she'd slighted without realizing it, and came up with nothing. She'd been the victim of a random break-in. The more she thought about it, the angrier she was. It wasn't bad enough they stole her one thing of value, they had to trash the place, as well? On its heels, another thought whispered through her consciousness and she hurried to the bedroom. A wave of nausea rolled over her when she saw her jewelry box overturned on the bureau.

"Oh, n-no. P-please be there," she whispered.

Most of her good jewelry had long since been pawned to pay Beck's hospital bills. She had only one piece left of value and she searched through a tangle of discount store earrings and bracelets, hoping beyond hope she'd find it. When she didn't, tears sprang to her eyes and a sense of overwhelming loss took hold of her. Stumbling back to the living room, she rifled through the chaos, found her telephone, and punched in 911.

"Nine-One-One, do you have an emergency?" a female voice asked.

"I n-need to report a r-robbery," she choked out.

"Alright, Ma'am, try to calm down and tell me what happened."

"I j-just got home from w-work and f-found my apartment trashed and ..." she sucked in a breath. "There are some things missing."

The dispatcher took her name and address and promised to send a patrol car as soon as possible. Sweeping pieces of broken pottery to the floor, Emma sank down onto the couch, trembling from the inside out. The laptop could be replaced, as could the food and her broken CDs. But her wedding ring ... that loss was absolute.

Feeling bitter and betrayed, she'd taken the ring off the day after Beck's funeral, vowing never to wear it again. Unable to give it up completely, she tucked it in her jewelry box, thinking some day she'd have the diamond reset into something less painful.

In the year since Beck's death she'd gotten good at burying her memories, had even told herself she'd managed to erase them completely, but in her current state of shock and confusion, a picture from the past forced its way to the surface.

It had been a perfect day, and Emma never wanted it to end. As the sun spent the last of its violet light, she and Beck sat on a bench, looking out over Lake Champlain, Beck's arm draped across her shoulders.

"Happy anniversary, baby," he said, giving her a squeeze.

Snuggling against him, she knew that no moment could or would ever be more fulfilling. Removing his arm, he reached in his pocket and pulled out a small velvet box.

"What's this?" she asked.

"Something I wanted to get you last year."

She opened it, hands trembling. Her breath caught hard as she stared at the wide gold band, a princess-cut diamond glittering in its center.

"Beck ... can we afford this?"

"That's not for you to worry about," he said, planting a kiss on her cheek.

"My God ... this diamond is bigger than Texas."

"It's as big as forever, babe. Just like our love."

She sat, tears streaming down her face, buried under a sudden avalanche of memories. Some time later there was a loud knock at the door and a stout, silver-haired police officer walked in. Looking around, he let out a low whistle.

"You doing alright, ma'am?"

Lifting tear-filled eyes to his, Emma nodded.

He picked his way through the rubble and came to sit beside her.

"Can you give me a list of what's missing?"

"They t-took my l-laptop. It was about t-two years old. And my w-wedding ring." Her voice caught. "Those were the only two things of v-value I had."

He jotted the information on a pad. "How long were you gone today?"

"All day. I l-left at around seven this m-m-morning. I had dinner with friends after work. I didn't get home until around t-ten."

"That makes it hard to pin down a time."

"Do you th-think I'll ever get my ring back?"

"You can keep your eye on the pawn shops. It's likely to turn up sooner or later," he said, but his expression told her another story.

He asked her a few more questions, all the while making notes in his pad.

"It's strange," Emma finally said. "It's almost l-like they were angry they didn't get more."

"This is the work of a typical drug addict. Sloppy. Pissed off." She shuddered. "Do you think they'll come b-back?"

"Probably not. I wouldn't advise staying here alone until you get that door fixed, though. Is there anyone you can call?"

•

"Wow! This place is a freaking dump."

Shane's frown deepened as Mick voiced the very words

that popped into his head the moment he pulled up in front of the decrepit old building Emma called home. He glanced down the length of the city block, taking in the bars, the abandoned businesses, the derelicts hanging out in the doorways. He turned off the engine, taking care to activate the truck alarm before he and Mick climbed out and walked toward the crumbling brownstone building.

He wouldn't have thought it possible the place could be uglier inside than out, but surveying the mildewed carpet and graffiti painted walls, he thought it a definite likelihood. At the end of a long, dimly lit hall, a door stood open, and he strode toward it, immeasurably pissed off and not quite sure why.

Inside, Emma sat on a battered sofa, and beside her, an old, gray-haired cop. A glance at her pale coloring and red-rimmed eyes made Shane's heart squeeze in his chest.

"Holy crap!"

"Are you alright, Emma?" he asked, ignoring Mick's rude appraisal of the situation.

She gave him a thin, wavering smile. "I'm a little shook up."

"I can imagine," he said, his eyes sweeping across the wreckage.

"You can't take it personally, ma'am," the cop said. "Like I told you, this was the handiwork of some lowlife, desperate druggie."

"They t-took my wedding ring," Emma said, her voice rising in anger. "It was all I had left of my husband. How can I not take that personally?"

She dissolved into tears and Shane felt like he'd been kicked in the gut. He ached to pull her into his arms, to comfort her, but all at once he felt like his feet were cemented to the floor.

Without a moment's hesitation Mick did what neither Shane nor the old cop could. Striding to her side, he dropped his arm around her, gently stroking her hair while she sobbed into his chest. As Shane watched the scene play out before him, he had never felt more admiration for his son. Or more jealousy.

"Guess I'll go around and talk to the neighbors," the officer said, heaving himself to his feet. "Though I doubt I'll get much out of them."

When he'd gone, Emma once again raised her tearful eyes to Shane. "I'm so s-sorry."

"For what?"

"For m-making you come back out so late." She forced a smile. "For being such a m-mess."

"There's no reason to be sorry. Have you got any garbage bags, any boxes?"

"My packing boxes are still under the bed. I wasn't p-planning on staying here that long. Just until I found something better."

Living in the subway station would be better, Shane thought.

"Good. Grab the garbage bags and Mick and I will start cleaning up this mess. Take the boxes and pack up anything that's still useable. You're moving out of here tonight."

"But I don't have anywhere to go."

"One of the cabins is vacant. I was planning to make some repairs on it this week. You can stay there until we figure something out."

"Shane, I could never afford that."

"Then pay me whatever it costs you to rent this place," he said gruffly. "Mick, go and get the boxes out from under the bed. It looks like we've got a long night ahead of us."

Chapter Six

It was after 2:00 AM when Emma's car rolled back into the parking lot at Shadow Lake, followed by Shane's truck laden with what was left of her earthly possessions. She stood, kneading her aching shoulders, as Shane retrieved a tarp from the storage shed and tied it down over the load.

"You can stay in the guest room for tonight," he told her. "We'll sort everything out in the morning."

Physically and emotionally drained, she thought the cabin had never looked more welcoming. He led her through the kitchen and down a short hallway, opening the second door on the left. Emma's exhausted brain registered luxurious chocolate-colored carpet, and a queen-sized sleigh bed with a multicolored quilt.

"Try and get some rest," he said, he said, giving her shoulders a gentle squeeze.

When the door closed behind him, she stripped off her clothes, lay down on the bed, and crashed into sleep, too emotionally wrecked to analyze the warm, tingling sensation she'd felt at his touch.

She awoke the next morning to sunlight streaming through the curtains and the happy shrieks of children at play. Rolling out of bed, she wrapped herself in the quilt and wandered to the window.

A pair of small, golden haired girls raced past, their beach pails swinging as they scampered to catch up with their laughing father.

"I d'wanna be a rotten egg, Daddy!"

"Daddy, wait!"

Smiling, she let the curtain fall back in place.

Padding down the hallway, she found the kitchen empty and

the coffee pot full. A glance at the clock told her she was already very late for work. She removed a coffee mug from the cupboard and poured it full, added cream and sugar, and took a long, grateful swallow.

"How'd you sleep?"

She turned at the sound of Shane's voice. He stood in the doorway, regarding her with a mixture of concern and something else, something evocative and vaguely unsettling. She clutched the quilt closer around her, all too aware she wore nothing underneath it. "Looks like I overslept."

"You had a rough night."

"But the store …"

"Mick's got the store covered. You're taking the day off."

"I can't take the day off. I just started—"

"You're taking the day off, Ms. Beckman, boss' orders. Now no more arguments, okay?"

He left her to a breakfast of cereal and fresh strawberries, returning again after she'd dressed in a pair of old jeans and a T-shirt.

Reaching in the cupboard, he retrieved an open can of coffee. "All of the cottages come equipped with coffee makers. This should hold you over until you can get to the store."

Touched by his thoughtfulness, she blinked back tears. Ten minutes later as they bumped down the path to the rows of cottages by the lake, Emma stole a glance at his profile. Was it her imagination, or was he even better looking than he'd been the day before? When they pulled up in front of the last cottage in the row, he gave her a heart-stopping smile. "Welcome home."

A lump formed in her throat. "Shane, I can't t-tell you how much I appreciate this."

Her gratitude seemed to embarrass him and he waved the words away. "No big deal. Come on, I'll show you around."

The front door opened into cozy living room warmed by honey pine walls and a cut stone fireplace. A bank of windows on the opposite wall provided a spectacular view of the lake. Off the living room was a kitchenette equipped with a refrigerator and a small gas stove. Across the hall she discovered a standard-issue bathroom, and adjoining it, a bedroom with chest of drawers and a stripped-down double bed. The cottage was far from fancy, but it was more of a home than she'd had in a year.

"Like I said, it needs some updating, but I think you'll be comfortable here for the time being," Shane commented, watching closely for her reaction.

"It's beautiful."

He stuffed his hands in his pockets and looked away. "Good, then. If you think it'll do, then I guess I'll start unloading the truck."

While Shane got busy with the boxes, Emma returned to the kitchen. She'd just started a pot of coffee when a high pitched squeal of laughter sent her to out to the deck. A teenaged girl in a fluorescent orange bikini top and a pair of cut off jeans ran down the sandy strip of beach, closely pursued by a boy of about sixteen. Beyond them, the lake sparkled beneath a cloudless sky. Emma stood for a long moment, breathing in the fresh, clean air until she heard the door slide open behind her.

"You'll want to watch your step out here," Shane said, coming up behind her. "The deck's got some rotted boards that need replacing."

His glance skimmed the lakefront, resting on the young boy and the girl in the bikini. Frowning, he cupped his hands around his mouth. "Hey, Alex?"

Turning, the boy peered at the cottage, one hand shielding his eyes against the sun. "S'up, boss?"

"Have you got those shower stalls done yet?"

"On my way."

As the boy ambled to a waiting golf cart, Shane sighed. "I get so tired of being the bad guy."

"But you're so good at it," Emma quipped.

Leaning on the railing, he gazed out at the water. "I think Mick's smoking."

"Oh, no."

"I found a lighter in his pocket when I was doing laundry last week, and two days ago I saw a wadded cigarette pack in the garbage. It's almost like he wanted me to find it."

"What's going on with him?"

"I don't know. He's become a different kid since his mother left."

"Do you want me to try and t-talk to him?"

"No. It's my responsibility. I'll deal with it."

Following him back inside, she saw his gaze sweep over her packing boxes.

"You're not much of a pack rat, are you?"

Kneeling beside a box, she peeled back a layer of masking tape. "I sold most everything after I lost my husband. I've found it's kind of liberating, living bare bones. Just think how bad I'd feel today if I'd had a big-screen TV and a killer stereo system in that apartment."

Pulling back the flaps, she retrieved the first item in the box, an eight-by-ten photo of her and Beck on their honeymoon. Setting it on the table, she returned to the box and pulled out a stack of dish towels.

Shane picked up the photo and studied it. "Is this your husband?"

"Yes, that's Beck."

"How long has he been ... gone?"

"He died a year ago."

"I'm sorry."

She nodded.

"What happened to him?"

"He had an accident." It was her standard answer for anyone who asked. She didn't tell him the rest, couldn't. "I think the coffee's probably ready. Want to join me for a cup?"

"I'd like to, but I really should get back to work. I've got a bazillion and one things to see to before the weekend."

•

Beating a hasty retreat from Emma's cottage, Shane wondered what on earth had possessed him to unload his baggage on her, and to want to take hers on his shoulders.

After Blair's betrayal he sealed himself off against emotions like love and affection, hurt, and yes, even desire. Telling himself he wouldn't be taken for a fool again, he erected thick brick walls around himself, walls he'd thought impenetrable.

But Emma was getting to him.

Vulnerable, beautiful Emma. In exactly three days time she'd broken through his barriers. She'd melted his resolve, toppled all of his well-thought-out arguments in favor of being alone, making him want things he had no business wanting. He'd failed at every relationship that mattered to him. And yet, one look into her gray eyes made him fool enough to want to try again.

•

With the last of her boxes unpacked, Emma drove into town to tie up some loose ends. She filled out a change of address form at the post office, canceled her phone and cable service at the apartment, and then went to pay a visit to her landlord. In between curse words, the crusty old man refused to return her security deposit, in the end soundly slamming the door in her face. Driving away, Emma heard the echo of Beck's voice in her head. *When are you going to start standing up for yourself, babe? You let people walk all over you ...*

He'd said it to her at least a hundred times, but aggressiveness wasn't in her nature. All her life she'd been a smooth-sailing dinghy in a crazy motorboat world. Still, she was angry with herself. Not so much that she'd allowed herself to be walked on, as that she'd wanted to give the security deposit to Shane as a down payment on her rent and car repairs. She drove away from the apartment building, promising herself she'd practice being more assertive.

After she'd phoned the insurance company about her laptop, she headed for the grocery store to pick up some staples for her new kitchen. She filled her cart with the basics — bread, milk, cheese, and then strolled through the produce aisle, selecting a cantaloupe and a quart of fresh berries.

The heavenly aroma of garlic shrimp drifted to her from the store's Market Café section, making her mouth water. In the first year of her marriage she scoured cookbooks for exotic recipes and spent countless hours in her half-finished kitchen learning how to prepare them to perfection. She hadn't gone all out to cook a meal in over a year because there hadn't seemed any point in preparing an elaborate meal just for herself. But now ... maybe she could dust off her cookbooks and invite Mick and Shane in for dinner, a well-deserved thank you for coming to her rescue last night. The thought pleased her and she decided to go for it.

Her taste buds cried out for crab quiche, but Shane seemed a bit more basic than that, so she decided on Lasagna Belmonte with Italian bread and a romaine salad with a lemon vinaigrette dressing. She smiled as she selected a package of sausage from the meat cooler, thinking how nice it would be to have a man to cook for again.

The thought was jolting and she sharply reprimanded herself. He's not your man, Emma, he's your boss. Get it straight.

Back home, she put her groceries away and walked up the path in search of Shane. She found him in the office, talking on the phone. Noticing her in the doorway, he motioned her inside.

"Wait, we decided on six-fifty." He sighed. "Alright. But that's as high as I'm going to go... Run that by me again?" Grabbing a pen from his desk, he scribbled the words *Grape Mineral Water—three cases* on a notepad. "Alright, I'll see what I can do." Hanging up the phone, he pushed out a breath. "Musicians."

"Are you having a concert?" she asked.

"Saturday night. It's supposed to be a kick-off to the summer season. The way they keep changing their rates, I hope to God I can still afford them by then. Did you get everything squared away in town?"

"Most everything." His gaze lingered on her for a long moment and she looked at the floor, all at once feeling shy. "That's sort of why I'm here. I'd like to invite you and Mick to come and have dinner with me tonight, if you don't already have plans. M-my way of saying thanks for last night."

"Mick's going out with friends for the evening," he said, adding softly, "but I'm free."

Her face grew warm. She'd counted on Mick's presence to make it feel more ... what? More not like a date?

"Then you'd better b-bring your appetite," she said, striving for nonchalance and she feared, failing badly. "Because I'm making a full pan of lasagna."

"Ooh," he groaned. "Now you're talking my language."

"I'll have it ready by six."

"Can we make it seven? I've got a clogged drain in shower three, and then I have a date with a leaky toilet seal."

"S-seven it is."

Back at the cottage, Emma indulged herself in a bubble bath, hoping to ease the tension she suddenly felt. Maybe it hadn't been wise to invite him after all. Maybe he'd get the wrong idea.

Why would it be so wrong? an inner voice asked.

As she thought about the implications, fear fisted in her stomach. "B-because it would, that's why," she murmured.

Stepping from the tub, she toweled her hair dry and slipped into her terry cloth robe. In the kitchen, she set about browning the sausage and slicing onions and peppers. With dinner well underway, she dragged the table out to the deck and set it up with a tablecloth and a set of white taper candles. Standing back to survey the scene, she quickly whisked the candles from the table, reminding herself she didn't want Shane to get the wrong idea, to think the invitation was anything other than a simple display of gratitude.

And is it, Emma? the small, worrisome voice persisted.

At six-thirty she slipped into the bedroom and changed into a pair of fawn colored slacks and a matching lace-trimmed camisole. She barely had time to pull her hair back into a clip and brush on a coat of mascara before a loud knock summoned her to the door. Stomach quivering, she hurried to open it.

Shane stood on the front porch, wearing a pair of jeans and a blue cotton shirt. His glance moved over her and she saw unmasked appreciation in his eyes before he handed her a bottle of wine. "My contribution," he said. "I hope I'm not too early."

"R-right on time," she said, still reeling from the wholly male appraisal in his eyes.

He followed her inside and she hurried to the kitchen to check on the lasagna. "So, what's Mick up to tonight?" she asked.

"He's at the movies. I figured I'd cut him some slack tonight. He's going to have his work cut out for him in the next few days. We all are."

While she tossed the salad, he told her about the concert he'd planned months in advance as a thank you to his regular guests and a drawing card for new business.

"Sam Valentino and the Rockets," he said. "They're sort of like Ozzy Osborne meets The Beach Boys."

"Interesting combination."

"They've promised to tone it down a notch, and throw in some patriotic songs in honor of the Memorial Day weekend. I've been dealing with their manager, Skye Blue. She's a real piece of work."

"Skye Blue?" Emma asked, grinning.

"I rest my case."

The timer rang and Emma pulled the lasagna from the oven. "That smells fantastic," Shane said. "What can I do to help?"

"You can carry the lasagna," she said, handing him a pair of oven mitts. "I thought we'd eat on the deck, since it's such a pretty n-night out."

"Good plan," he said, picking up the steaming pan. Emma grabbed the salad and the plate of Italian bread and followed him out to the deck. When they were seated, Shane picked up the spatula and carved two thick wedges from the pan of lasagna, depositing one on each of their plates. She watched anxiously as he popped a forkful into his mouth, not relaxing until she saw his pleased expression.

"This is fantastic, Emma."

"It's one of my specialties."

"So what you're telling me then is you're not only beautiful, but talented, too?"

Blushing profusely, she took a swallow of wine. "Tell me more about opening weekend."

"The campers should start pulling in here tomorrow afternoon, and then it will be nonstop. You'll be busting your tail in the store for all of Friday. After you close up, we'll have to set up the rec hall for the dance. I'm hoping you can give the boys a hand with the decorating. I'm thinking red, white and blue streamers, maybe some glittery stars."

"Sounds like you've got it pretty well planned."

"We've been doing the concerts for about five years now, but it never seems to get any less stressful. Anyway," he grinned, "let's not talk about business."

Despite Mick's absence, the conversation flowed easily. They talked about the campground, and about Emma's brief, disastrous tenure at the applesauce factory. As she related the story to Shane, it actually seemed humorous and she found herself laughing more than she had in a year. Dusk turned to darkness as they drank wine and chatted like they'd known each other forever, rather than just a few days. Emma was lulled by the hushing sound of the lake, and the deep, rich rhythms of Shane's voice. It felt right, natural somehow, that they were spending the evening together. Finally, reluctantly, she stood to clear away the plates. Shane followed her to the kitchen, stacking the dishes in the sink while she put away the leftover food.

"I meant to get the place painted before I rented it out again," he told her apologetically.

"I don't worry too much about cosmetics," Emma said. "Beck and I bought a fixer-upper when we were first married. I put everything I had into the place. Spent four years painting walls and refinishing hardwood floors just so the new owners could put down carpet and hang wallpaper. I've l-learned not to get too attached to places."

Shane regarded her thoughtfully. "Do you want to talk about him?"

For twelve months Emma had held it in. The pain and anger, the guilt, because who would she have confided in? Certainly not her mother. And after Beck died her friends drifted away, lost in their own guilt and embarrassment. For twelve long, lonely months she'd ached for release, for someone to give a damn, for the ability to speak freely. And now that the opportunity presented itself at last, she found she couldn't.

"You can if you want to," he said, strong, gentle hands kneading her shoulders. His kindness undid her more than his gruffness ever could and she felt her eyes brimming with tears.

"Hey." Cupping her face in his hands, he forced her to meet his eyes. "I'm sorry, Emma. I shouldn't have asked." Strong, gentle fingers wiped away her tears before resting tenderly on her cheek.

"You probably think all I do is cry."

"You can do that, too, sweetheart. Believe me, I know what it is to cry."

He gathered her up in his arms and held her. Her head knew it was inappropriate, but her heart ached for the comfort of his arms and when his lips touched down on hers, she was too needy to do anything but respond.

He moaned softly as the kiss deepened, one hand pulling her closer to the core of his own need, the other caressing her bare shoulders. When his hands found their way beneath the fabric of her camisole, a jolt of white hot desire brought her sharply to her senses.

"Shane, we shouldn't be d-doing this."

"Let me make it better, Emma," he whispered into her hair. "Let me stay with you tonight."

Warm waves of desire rushed through her, but in the end her fear won out. If Beck left her, then this man would, too. Loving

Shane Lucy would lead to nothing but sorrow, and she knew that one more ounce of sorrow, one more salty tear would drown her. The sheer terror of enduring that kind of pain again made her strong and she firmly pushed him away.

"I c-can't," she said. "I'm sorry if you misunderstood, if you thought t-tonight was an invitation for anything more than dinner. Because it w-wasn't."

His eyes searched hers for a moment, and she saw pain, and disappointment, and finally, anger.

"My mistake," he said coolly. Dropping his hands from her shoulders, he walked out the door and disappeared into the darkness.

Chapter Seven

A busy morning in the store left Emma little time to dwell on the fiasco of the night before. It seemed she'd no more than unlocked the door before the trucks started rolling in, bringing gallons of ice cream and nutty bars, bagged ice, and fresh baked donuts. Emma checked the items against her purchase orders as the drivers unloaded the merchandise.

At midmorning a large box truck pulled into the lot and Shane seemed to appear from out of nowhere. He guided the truck in, then hung around to help the driver offload the cases of beer and soft drinks. He didn't spare Emma a word, or even so much as a glance, and she knew his anger from the previous night hadn't softened.

She busied herself with restocking the shelves, seeing to customers, and checking in the occasional camper. When things slowed down enough for her to catch her breath, she gathered up the boxes and packing materials from the deliveries and carried them out back to the dumpster. Shane was tinkering with his riding lawnmower and didn't even look up when she passed. She felt a twinge of regret. You picked a heck of a time to start asserting yourself, Emma, she thought.

She'd expected the cold shoulder from him, had even prepared for it. It was human nature to be bad-tempered when things didn't go your way, especially when it came to sex. But there was more to it than that. Last night, tossing restlessly in her bed, she couldn't help remembering his tenderness and his plea not to turn him away, and she realized that in his own way Shane was just as needy as she was. He'd lost his partner, too. Not to death, as she had, but Blair's absence from Shane's life was just as final as Beck's was from hers. He'd reached out to her for comfort, and blinded by her own fears, she'd shut him out.

She walked in the back door just as Mick entered through the front.

"Sorry I'm so late getting you your lunch break. This is the first chance I've had to get away."

"Not a problem, Mick," she said. "I'm not very hungry today anyway."

He grabbed a bottle of juice from the cooler. "Man, it seems like he's just looking for extra stuff for me to do today. He's being a total jerk."

"Well, it has been pretty crazy around here today."

He snorted. "You ain't seen nothing yet, Miss Emma."

Grabbing a bottle of juice for herself, she joined him on the porch. "How was the movie last night?"

His eyes met hers before he dropped them to the floor. "It was alright."

Emma got the distinct feeling Mick was lying about something, but for what reason she couldn't fathom. "Just alright?"

He shrugged. "I've seen better."

"At least you got to go out though, right? Spend some time hanging out with your friends and being unproductive?"

She'd hoped to jolly him out of his bad mood, but he merely shrugged. She sat in silence for a moment, until another thought occurred to her. She knew it was none of her business but she'd grown fond of Mick in a very short time and she felt compelled to look out for him.

"Mick," she ventured, "I hope you haven't started smoking cigarettes."

His head whipped in her direction. "Why would you say that?"

"You smell like smoke, dude."

"It's probably from raking out the campfire rings."

She sipped her juice, not answering.

"Okay, I smoke once in awhile. It helps me de-stress."

"Mmm."

"You're not going to tell my dad, are you? He'll tweak."

"If I've smelled it, he probably has, too."

"Great."

"It's really bad for you, ya know?"

"So is fast food, but everyone eats it."

She was searching her mind for a reply when Shane drove past in the truck.

"Did you see that?" Mick muttered. "He didn't even look at us. What a jerk"

Beneath his words she sensed a deep hurt which he'd converted to the safer form of anger. Like father, like son, she thought. Her heart broke for him, because she understood the pain of living with a parent's displeasure, of feeling like everything she did was wrong. Years after the fact she still bore the emotional scars of Miranda's scorn. Mick was much more resilient than she'd been at his age, but even so, she ached to reassure him, to explain that Shane's anger was not directed at him, but at her. But there would be no getting out of that conversation gracefully, so she said instead, "He's just stressed about opening weekend, Mick. He's got an awful lot on his mind."

"And I don't, right?"

His cell phone rang, precluding an answer. Flipping it open, Mick stood and ambled across the parking lot, out of her earshot. Swallowing the last of her juice, Emma headed back inside.

•

Shane felt like a damned fool. Thankfully he had more to do that day than a man could accomplish in a week, so he didn't have to interact with her, or even think about her. Yeah, right.

He drove past the store and out of the lot, being careful not to glance in her direction. Memories of the previous night came back in all of their humiliating clarity. They'd shared a good meal and good conversation. He should have left well enough alone. Why had he pushed the envelope?

He knew the answer, of course. Because once he held her in his arms there was no turning back. Blair had been cold to him for so long he'd forgotten what it felt like to hold a warm-blooded woman. And then along came Emma, with her teardrops and lace, making him fool enough to think he could be needed and wanted again. Remembering how eagerly she returned his kiss, he felt the ache of longing. It was quickly followed by a spark of anger. The attraction went both ways. He was sure of it. Why, at the last moment, did she refuse to act on it? Women.

He should have stuck to his guns, kept his walls intact. Thank God she'd only loosened a brick or two. He'd have them repaired in no time.

•

Having confronted Mick about the smoking, Emma hadn't expected to see him for the rest of the day, so she was surprised, at four o'clock, when he bounded back into the store. "Hey, Miss Emma. Can I get some petty cash from the bag?"

She made a pass at the ice cream cooler with a wet wipe, erasing a dozen small handprints. "Help yourself."

Rummaging in the bag, he removed two twenties. "I have to run down to the party store and pick up some new streamers and decorations. I can't find last years' in the storage room. I guess we must have junked them."

They chatted for a moment about the concert before Mick sprinted off on his mission. An hour later she emptied the wastebaskets and locked up the store. Seeing the office door open, she set the garbage bags on the front porch, pulled in a breath for courage, and walked across the lot.

Shane was seated behind the desk, making notes in one of his ledgers.

"I thought I should b-bring the bank bag over here," she told him. "It's pretty full today."

"Lock it in the file cabinet, then," he said, not looking up.

She slid open the drawer and deposited the bag inside. Pushing out another breath, she ventured, "Sh-shane, about yesterday ..."

He glanced up. "What about it?"

"I feel like there's a rift between us now."

"There's no rift. I was out of line. It won't happen again."

"I hope we can put it past us and still have a good w-working relationship."

"It's already forgotten," he said, but the chipped ice texture of his voice told Emma it wasn't.

With nothing left to do or say, she returned to the store and grabbed the bags of garbage from the porch. She carried them around back and heaved opened the dumpster. Beneath the packing debris she'd thrown out that morning, she caught a glimpse of a glittering silver star. Frowning, she pushed the packing debris aside and pulled out a large oblong box. Tearing back the flaps, she saw that it held a collection of glittery stars and more than a dozen rolls of red, white, and blue streamers.

Chapter Eight

Friday morning arrived early, with a commotion of barking dogs and crying babies. Curious, Emma dragged herself out of bed and padded to the window. Down on the beach, a man tossed a Frisbee for an eager Labrador retriever. She watched, smiling, as the dog bounded into the water after the sailing object, his joyous barking echoing across the lake.

Wrapping herself in her robe, she moved to the kitchen, prepared an extra-strong cup of coffee, and carried it out to the deck. The sun had barely bruised the morning sky, but even so, the campground hummed with activity. A sixty-something man in a blue sweat suit coaxed breakfast from the grill next door while his silver-haired wife sat on the deck, cradling a disconsolate baby. On the lakefront several men perched on the docks, fishing poles in hand, while a half-dozen sailboats already dotted the water. The air was permeated with a happy, holiday feel and Emma felt her spirits begin to lift.

As Shane predicted, the glorious weather brought people out of hibernation. By nine o'clock the lot was already backed up with campers, and by ten, the store swarmed with people picking up last-minute items as they set up their temporary home sites. Feeling in a state of perpetual motion, Emma took their money and answered countless questions about the campground and the area attractions. At mid-afternoon she was sitting behind the counter enjoying a lull in the chaos and a cool bottle of grape soda when the door opened and a man walked in. His glance moved around the store before he ambled up to the counter, preceded by the mingled odors of sweat and alcohol. Emma's glance flicked from his torn, dirty jeans to the leather do rag that covered his long, greasy ponytail.

"Can I help you?" she asked.

"You're not the little girl that was in here last week," he said.

"No, I'm not."

"Where'd the other little gal go?"

"She quit. Is there s-something I can help you with?"

"She quit, huh? Damn. I was hoping to meet her here today." His gaze crept over Emma, inch by inch, reminding her of the leering stares of her former co-workers at the applesauce factory and she felt her skin start to crawl.

"You're cuter than she was anyway," he said, his words slurring slightly. Turning back to her magazine, Emma flipped a page, hoping that if she ignored him he'd go away.

"What time do you get off work, sweetheart?" He leaned across the counter, entirely too close for her comfort. Her hand crept to the two-way radio on her belt and she reminded herself that help was no more than a flip of the switch away. She was seriously considering calling out an S.O.S. when the door opened again and a short, stout woman with flamboyant red hair strode inside. She was a welcome, if strange, diversion and Emma greeted her enthusiastically. "Hello, can I help you?"

"I sure hope so, honey," the woman said in a deep, throaty voice. "I'm looking for my man, Shane Lucy."

Emma took in the woman's kitschy rhinestone tube top and the rows of hoops that glittered from her eyebrows and wondered what on earth such a creature would want with Shane.

"Will I do?" the man asked, ogling her ample chest.

She gave him a hard stare. "Put your eyes back in your head, toots. I'm here on business."

"Your business could be my pleasure, if you know what I mean," he said.

"Honey, I got a feeling I'm twice the man you are, and more woman than you can handle, so be a good boy and go find someone else to aggravate."

Seeing the man's bemused expression, Emma snickered.

"Go on now," the woman said, flapping her hands in the general direction of the door. The man glared at her for a long moment and Emma's finger hesitated over the button on the two-way radio. To her relief, he turned on his heel and stalked away.

"What a creep," the redheaded woman said. "So, is Shane

around?"

"I can page him for you. Who should I say is asking?"

She slapped a business card on the counter with a flourish. "Skye Blue at your service."

Emma made the call. When Shane arrived moments later, Skye's wide, red lips broke into a grin. "Hey, babe. I thought I'd pop in and see where my boys are going to be playing tomorrow." She brazenly eyed him from head to toe. "My goodness, aren't you a tall drink of water."

Emma bit her lip to keep from giggling, and Shane shot her an annoyed glance. "The rec hall is right next door," he told Skye. "You're more than welcome to look around."

"Lead the way, babe." Emma watched, still biting her lip as linking her arm through his, Skye propelled him out the door.

•

"Nice place you've got here, babe."

"Thanks." He managed a smile, despite the grumblings of his inner voice. A million things to do today, and I'm stuck playing host to this red-headed Tasmanian She-Devil.

She'd detained him for nearly an hour in the rec hall, making outrageous last-minute demands, as if her two-bit band was accustomed to selling out major concert halls. Then she'd insisted on a tour of the campground. Nearly at the end of his patience, Shane had agreed to give her the abbreviated version. Skye Blue was a certifiable pain in the keester, but he had to admit, her blatant compliments were a salve for his bruised ego.

He drove past the cottages and up a small knoll to the playground where a man pushed a small boy on a swing. Hearing the boy's shrieks of excitement, he felt a pang. Mick had been gone much longer than he should have been last night and Shane wondered what his son was up to. He'd said he was going to make a trip to the party store for new decorations and then a stop at the pizza place for a bite to eat. Shane had expected him home at around seven o'clock, eight at the latest. Definitely not ten-thirty. He hadn't made a federal case out of it, deciding to cut the kid some slack. Still, he hated that Mick had become so secretive.

He remembered a time not so long ago when they'd been best buddies and Mick's constant stream of chatter had annoyed him. He thought with regret of the little boy who used to study and imitate his every move and he wondered if that Mick was still there somewhere, buried beneath the mohawk and the attitude.

The tour completed, he steered the golf cart back into the main lot and Skye heaved herself out. "I gotta hand it to you, babe, this is one of the nicest campgrounds I've seen."

"Thanks."

The door of the General Store opened and Emma appeared on the porch, looking so hot in a pair of white shorts and a black tank top it put his senses on red alert.

"Have you got a minute, Shane?" she asked.

"I suppose so," he said, feigning impatience. "What do you need?"

"The caterer brought the goodies for tomorrow night. I put the cakes in the cooler, but I'm not sure what to do with the rest of it."

"I'll have Mick come by later and pick it up. I have another cooler in the house."

"Okay." He watched, nearly salivating, as she turned and walked back inside.

"Thanks for the tour, babe," Skye said. "The boys will probably be here around two o'clock tomorrow to start setting up, if that's okay."

"I'll look forward to it," he said.

"If the weather holds I might just come with them and bring my swimsuit. That lake looks mighty inviting. Maybe we could take a dip together."

"I'm going to be swamped with work. Doubt I'll have the time, but you're welcome to it. 'Bye now." He fired up the golf cart and drove away quickly before she could detain him further.

•

Emma glanced up when Skye re-entered the store.

"M-m-mmm. Now that is one fine-looking hunk of a man," she said, peeking out the window for a last glimpse.

Not sure how to respond, Emma remained silent.

"What I wouldn't give..." The other woman sized Emma up. "But it looks like I came in a day late and a dollar short this time, didn't I?"

"Excuse me?"

"The man's head over heels crazy about you."

Emma nearly choked. "Why do you say that?"

She cracked a smile. "Call it a vibe, honey."

She grabbed a bottle of soda from the cooler, popped off the cap, and guzzled it down. With a satisfied belch, she set the empty bottle on the counter and breezed from the store.

At five o'clock, Emma locked up the building, dropped the bank bag in the office, and headed home for a shower and a quick bite to eat. All around her the campground buzzed with activity. In the picnic area, families sat down to grilled hot dogs and hamburgers, while on the lawn a cluster of men kidded each other good-naturedly as they played horseshoes, cans of beer in their hands. Along the beach, women in various stages of undress soaked up the last rays of the sun while jet skis cut frothy paths across the lake. The jollity around her was contagious and Emma found herself humming as she walked.

After a shower and a plate of cold lasagna she dressed in a pair of faded jeans and one of Beck's old Buffalo Bills sweatshirts and headed back to the rec hall, where Mick and Alex already had the ladders out.

"Wow, you guys don't mess around," Emma greeted them.

Mick shrugged. "If we finish up early enough, I'm hoping my dad will let me go out tonight."

"Got a date?" Emma asked.

"Nah." He shot a glance at Alex. "We're just going to hang out for awhile."

"Well then, let's get cracking, shall we?"

Emma put the two boys to work stringing red, white and blue streamers from the trusses while she retrieved a package of stars and began to hang them from the beams in groups of two and three. When all the packages were empty, she draped the buffet table with a red and white cloth and fashioned a blue crepe paper garland along the sides. An hour later the three stood back to admire their handiwork.

"It doesn't even look like the same place," Alex commented. "This is way better than it looked last year."

Mick dropped his arm around Emma's shoulders and squeezed. "Miss Emma, you rock."

"I couldn't have done it without you, dude," she said, giving him a shove.

"You all did an excellent job." At the sound of Shane's voice,

Emma's stomach clenched. "Now why don't you get out of here. You guys have done enough work for one day."

Seizing the moment, Mick asked, "Can I go downtown with Alex?"

"What's your plan, Stan?"

"We're just gonna hang out in the arcade. I'll be home by eleven."

"Ten."

"Alright."

"No messing around, right?"

"Right."

"Have fun."

As the two teens hurried away, Shane turned to Emma. "I think we're pretty well set for tomorrow night. I'd like to have you man the food table during the concert, if you don't mind."

"Not at all."

An awkward moment passed, and then Shane said, "Why don't you go home and get some rest. I think we're all gonna need it."

Later that night Emma sat on her deck, sipping a glass of wine and enjoying the stars and the blanket of quiet that seemed to wrap itself around Shadow Lake. It had been a long, exhausting day. Her thoughts skimmed over the dreadful man with the ponytail before finding their way back to Shane. His tone was brisk but at least he was speaking to her again. Not exactly the tenor of a man who was head over heels crazy about someone, she thought. She smiled, thinking that Skye Blue's vibe was badly in need of a tune up.

Chapter Nine

Saturday morning brought overcast skies and a steady, drizzling rain that dampened the festive atmosphere of the day before. Emma sat in her living room, drinking her morning coffee as she gazed out at the deserted stretch of lakefront, not a Frisbee or a sailboat in sight. The dampness in the air brought a chill to the little cottage and she thought how lovely it would be to have a fire crackling in the grate. It was the kind of cold, dreary morning when she and Beck would have stayed in bed, making slow, sweet love. The memory was painful and she quickly pushed it from her mind. Would she ever be rid of the ghosts that seemed to hover, ever on the periphery of her subconscious? Draining the last of the coffee from her cup, she moved to the bathroom to get ready for the day ahead.

The inhospitable weather kept most of the guests holed up in their campers, with only a handful of permanents stopping by the store for their morning coffee and newspapers. Emma worked her way down her list of preparations for the concert, carrying bags of party plates, plastic silverware and napkins to the rec hall and checking to make sure the red, white, and blue cakes had survived their night in the cooler. She didn't catch so much as a glimpse of Shane all morning, but the crackling of the two-way radio told her he was busy cleaning up fallen tree limbs down in area three.

By mid-morning the rain was falling steadily. Thunder rumbled through the valley, discouraging even the bravest of guests from venturing outside, so Emma decided it would be the perfect time to organize the storage room. She removed several old, dusty boxes of sales pads and register tape from the shelving units in the corner and was considering how to best make use of the space when above the steady pounding of rain she heard the bell above the front door announce a visitor. Wiping her hands on her jeans, she headed out front to greet her customer.

She saw the man with the pony tail and do-rag standing at the front counter and her heart sank. For a moment she considered hiding out in the storage room and avoiding him altogether, but how silly would that be? She couldn't very well hide from him all summer. Better to see what he wanted and hopefully send him on his way.

You're going to start being more assertive, Emma, she reminded herself. Squaring her shoulders, she marched out front to greet him.

"There's my girl," he said, his words slightly slurring. "Now what were you doing hiding out back?" He advanced a step closer and she detected the familiar odors of sweat and alcohol.

"Is there s-something I can help you with?" she asked, cursing her stutter for giving away her nervousness.

He gave her a sly grin. "Oh, there's not a doubt in my mind about that, sweetheart."

Emma's anger flared. "Look, I'm awfully busy, so if you'll just tell me what it is you'd like, I'll g-get it for you."

He advanced a step closer, nearly stumbling over his own feet. "You don't look so busy to me. I thought maybe you'd like a little company."

"M-maybe you'd better get yourself a cup of coffee." She stopped just short of adding, you look like you could use some sobering up.

"Now that's more like it." His hand whispered across the space between them and rested on her arm. "We'll sit and have a nice cup of coffee together, get to know each other a little bit better."

She moved her arm away. "Please don't touch me."

"Aww, come on," he whined. "I just wanted to see if you were as soft as you look."

Fear mingled with anger, causing Emma to tremble inside. "I think it would be best if you l-left now."

"You're tossing me out?"

"Yes, I guess I am."

"I'm a good customer here," he said, his voice rising in belligerence. "You can't throw me out."

"Sir, I think—"

"I can't believe this!" His voice escalated to a shout and Emma flinched. The man obviously wasn't playing with a full deck. "I'm gonna tell you something, sweetheart, nobody talks to me like that, not when I'm paying good money to stay someplace."

"I think your stay here is about over, Dusty."

Emma whirled at the sound of Shane's voice. He stood in the doorway of the storage room, his gaze resting firmly, but not unkindly, on the derelict man.

"Aww, come on, Shane. I didn't mean any harm."

"I talked to you about this last week. I thought I made myself clear then."

"You were the one who said I could stay."

"I said you could stay if you'd behave yourself. It doesn't look to me like you're keeping up your end of the deal."

"I just came in to get a cup of coffee, man. She wouldn't let me have it."

"Get your coffee, then, and I'll have Mick drive you back to town."

"Aww, come on, Shane."

"Or I could call the Sheriff and have him come and pick you up. Your choice."

The man's shoulders slumped in defeat. "No need to call the cops. I'll go with Mick."

Shane made a call on his two-way radio while Dusty filled a coffee cup with badly shaking hands. Moments later Mick pulled up in front of the store and laid on the horn.

"Before you go, I think you owe this lady an apology," Shane said.

"Sorry I bothered you, ma'am" he mumbled, eyes cast downward as he stumbled out the door. When it closed behind him, Emma slumped back against the wall.

"Are you okay?" Shane asked.

"I'm f-fine."

"I'm sorry about that. I guess I forgot to warn you about Dusty."

"Who is he?"

"When I was growing up he was my father's right and left hands around here. Now he's a homeless bum."

"What happened to him?"

Shane sighed. "His daughter drowned in a boating accident about eight years ago. Shortly after that his wife left him. Things fell apart pretty quickly for Dusty after that. I set him up with a little campsite down by the lake. I let him hang around and do odd jobs when he's sober enough. It gives him a break from the homeless shelter."

Emma shuddered at the thought of the dismal gray building that squatted beside the river on Warner Avenue, surrounded by vacant storefronts and abandoned factories.

"Now I feel bad," she said.

"No need to feel bad. He'll sober up and come back in a few days. Then we'll try it again. If he gets out of line, out he goes. That's our deal and he knows it."

"I'm glad you showed up when you did. I don't know if I could have handled him on my own."

"He's usually pretty harmless. You just have to be firm with him."

He smiled at her and Emma couldn't help the strange fluttering in her chest. He looked sexy and disheveled with his beard-stubbled chin, his hair curling damply on his collar. Her gaze traveled to his wet clothing, taking in the way his jeans fit snugly around his thighs and the fluttering sensation increased.

"You're s-soaked through. Let me get you a cup of coffee," she said, averting her gaze. She poured a steaming cup and handed it to him and he took a swallow. "You look tired, Shane."

"It's been one thing after another today. I'll be glad when this weekend's over." He looked as though he might say more, but instead he gave her a smile that turned her inside out. "I should go and put on some dry clothes. Thanks for the coffee."

•

She was absolutely lovely, but what he felt went much deeper than mere physical attraction. Shane stood beneath the hot spray of the shower, thinking about the alarming effect Emma had on him, body and soul. He'd told himself he was immune to her, that he was doing just fine before she showed up, and would continue to be fine long after she was gone. But one look at her and his resolve to stay away crumbled.

He'd been on his way home for a shower and a change of clothes when he heard the angry shouting coming from inside the store.

He hadn't known exactly what was going on, only that he needed to protect Emma from it, whatever it was. It frightened him just how strong that instinct was.

He sighed. He was going to have to do something about Dusty, but what? He'd warned the man as sternly as he knew how, and Shane didn't have the heart to ban him from the campground altogether. Not when so much of Dusty's history was tangled up in his. He stepped from the shower and toweled off, unable to shake his memories of the younger, kinder man Dusty had once been.

Twelve years his senior, Dusty had been like an older brother when Shane was growing up. It was Dusty who taught him how to drive the dump truck, and how to unclog a stubborn drain. He'd he taught Shane the ins and outs of the campground and covered for him more than once when he screwed up, sparing Shane many a tongue lashing from his father. Shane had looked up to Dusty, admired him. And now he was a drunken bum.

Dusty Martin was living proof of how life could chew a man up and spit him out in an instant. And what's more, Shane knew he himself could have easily caved under the hand of fate, given in to the temptation of alcohol and its sweet oblivion, if he hadn't had a business to run and a son to set an example for.

His troubled thoughts turned to Mick. As much as Blair's betrayal had hurt him, it had devastated his son. Overnight, Mick had changed from a fun-loving, even-tempered kid into an angry and often hostile young man. The only time Shane caught a glimpse of the old Mick any more was when he was around Emma, and Shane knew that Mick needed Emma's sweet, calming presence in his life as much as he did. Losing Blair had left them both vulnerable, wide open for a woman with a soft voice and a kind spirit. A woman with a heart of gold and a will of iron. A woman like Emma.

He thought of the kiss they'd shared and his body reacted violently. He reminded himself she wasn't his to love. Not yet. He'd have to wait until she came to him. And wait he would, even if it took forever.

●

By late afternoon the storm clouds had rolled away, replaced by a golden sun and the promise of a cool, clear evening. The band arrived at two o'clock as promised and was now practicing loudly in the rec hall, overseen by an effervescent Skye Blue in a neon orange mini skirt and a pair of matching stiletto heels.

At five o'clock Emma exchanged her jeans and tee shirt for a white tank dress, ran a brush through her hair, and headed back to the rec hall. Shane had ordered enough pizza and chicken wings for a small city, and Emma saw that not a bit of it was going to waste. Mick and Alex were camped out by the food table, along with several of the band members and two off-duty cops Shane had hired to handle crowd control for the evening.

With the feast consumed, Emma cleared away the pizza boxes and paper plates and began setting up the refreshment table for the concert. She and Mick had just brought over the last of the baked goods when the guests started to arrive.

The band opened with a rendition of Bruce Springsteen's *Born in the USA*, causing the rec hall to erupt in cheers and whistles. When they followed with a number by C.C.R. a mob of teenagers thronged to the dance floor, while adults in cut-off jeans and tie dyed tops sang along, alternately clapping their hands and drinking their wine coolers.

Emma watched, smiling, as she served plates of cake and poured glasses of lemonade. Her smile faded with a glance at the back door, where Mick and Shane were deep in discussion. A look at their faces told Emma it wasn't a pleasant one. Moments later, when Mick stormed from the rec hall, Emma slipped away from the banquet table and followed.

He strode down the path and was nearly to the beach before she caught up with him.

"Hey, Mick?"

He stopped walking, but didn't turn around.

"What?"

"Are you okay?"

"I'm great."

"It seemed like you left in kind of a hurry."

"He's such a jackass. I can't stand to be around him any more."

She drew a deep breath, not even sure now why she'd followed or what she hoped to accomplish. "I know it's a hard time for you right now, Mick. But you have to t-try and remember your dad's having a hard time, too."

"Stop covering for him, Emma. You don't know how he really is."

He pushed out a breath, angrily scrubbing at the tears that formed on his lashes. "He won't let me do anything. It's like he thinks I'm a freaking preschooler or something."

"I can imagine that's pretty frustrating."

"It's hell. I can't wait until I turn eighteen so I can get out of this dump."

Emma's heart wept because Mick's words echoed her exact sentiments at his age. "I know it's tough, Mick," she said softly. "But hang in there. Things will get better."

"He makes me feel like such a screw-up. Like he has room to talk." He turned to her, misery etched into his face. "He had to marry my mom, did you know that?"

"N-no, I didn't."

"She got pregnant when she was barely older than I am now. She couldn't keep her legs closed, and sixteen years later she turned around and blamed him for tying her down. So she took off and now he blames me." Angry tears spilled down his cheeks.

"I doubt that very much."

"Well I don't."

She put her arm around him and drew him close, allowing him the freedom to cry. "I think you need to sit down and talk to him about some of this stuff," she finally said.

"It won't do any good."

"You might be surprised."

He wiped his eyes with the back of his hand. "Thanks for, you know, listening. The thing is, I think I want to be alone for awhile."

"Find me later if you want to talk some more."

She watched as he disappeared into the shadows. Walking back to the rec hall, she contemplated the situation and wondered what, if anything, she could do to help. Her heart was heavy with sorrow and she wondered how it was possible that she'd become so emotionally entangled in this family in such a short amount of time.

•

"So anyway, that's when I decided that if I couldn't make it in a band I could damn sure promote the hell out of one. You listening to me, Babe?"

Shane brought his attention sharply back to Skye Blue. Her gaze was fixed intently on his face and he realized he hadn't heard a word she said.

"Interesting," he said.

She grinned. "You could just go over there, you know. It would save you the stiff neck you're gonna have tomorrow from craning it all night."

Busted.

"I own the place, Skye. It's my job to make sure everyone has enough to eat."

She rolled her eyes. "Uh-huh."

Good God, was he that transparent? Despite himself, his gaze traveled back to the food table where Emma was acting the perfect hostess. His eyes caressed her white dress, her sun-kissed skin. No woman has a right to look that good, he thought. Her smile lit up the room, and he couldn't help noticing the men who crowded around her, wanting some of that sweet light for themselves.

The band launched into a popular Nickelback song and the crowd of teenagers whooped. Shane shifted his gaze to the dance floor, hoping for a glimpse of a green Mohawk with no such luck. He probably should have allowed Mick to invite Danielle. It would have prevented another row, and God knew another altercation with his son was the last thing he needed tonight.

After their ugly words he'd let Mick leave, thinking he'd give him time to cool off. He glanced at his watch. He'd thought Mick would have returned by now.

•

Her feet throbbed, her head ached, and her face literally hurt from smiling. By ten o'clock, with most of the food consumed, Emma stepped outside for a breath of fresh air. The night was cool and clear and a breeze whispered through the campground, lending welcome relief from the airless heat of the rec hall.

"Taking a break?"

She turned when Shane emerged from the shadows.

"It's getting pretty warm in there." She fanned her face with her hand. "But the band's doing an excellent job. Everyone seems to be having fun. Especially the teens and 'tweens."

"Speaking of teens, have you seen Mick lately?"

"No. Not for awhile."

"I've been calling him on the radio, but he's not answering."

"Maybe he's out taking a breather somewhere."

"We had an argument earlier. I was pretty hard on him. Maybe I'll go and take a look around, see if I can find him."

Without waiting to be invited, Emma fell into step beside him.

They found the cabin dark, and after a quick search proved it to be empty, they walked down to the lakefront. Not finding him there, they checked the alley behind the store. The door to the utility barn stood open and Emma saw a gaping hole where the truck should have been. Inside, Mick's two-way radio crackled on a shelf. Shane picked it up and turned the dial until the crackling ceased. "I guess this explains why he's not answering. I can't believe he'd take the truck without asking."

Fishing his cell phone from his pocket, he punched in Mick's number and listened intently. "Voicemail," he said, disconnecting the call.

"I wonder where he went," Emma said.

"I don't know. But he's in for a world of hurting when he gets back."

"He probably d-didn't go far. Maybe he just needed to drive a little, clear his head. I do that sometimes."

"Don't make excuses for him, Emma. He snuck out of here hoping I wouldn't notice. In my truck, no less. There's no reason good enough for that kind of defiance."

"Shane, m-maybe you and Mick should—"

"Babe? Oh, there you are." Skye Blue wobbled toward them on her high heels. "The boys are about to do a ladies' choice number. I want you to be my dance partner, and I won't take no for an answer."

She grabbed his hand and dragged him back to the rec hall. Emma followed, promising herself she'd pin him down later and make him listen to what she had to say.

•

By midnight the party was winding down. The adults were yawning in their beer and only a handful of teenagers still dotted the dance platform. Skye Blue had Shane corralled by the makeshift stage, flapping her hands as she talked. Emma couldn't help noticing the tension in his stance or the way his gaze kept drifting to the parking lot.

The band had just launched into their last song of the night when Emma heard screeching brakes and the unmistakable sound of metal crunching against metal outside. When Shane stormed from the rec hall, she crept cautiously behind him.

She winced when she reached the lot. The truck sat beside a dented sign, its headlight broken and dangling. The radio blared rap music and a dazed looking Mick sat behind the wheel. Shane strode to the truck.

"Where have you been?" he demanded.

"Out for a ride."

"Have you been drinking?"

"A little."

"You've been drinking and driving? In my truck?"

Mick shrugged. "It looks that way."

A muscle twitched in Shane's jaw and Emma could see tethered fury in his eyes. Yanking open the door, he reached inside and dragged Mick out, catching him as he stumbled to the ground. He glared at him for a long moment before giving him a small shove. "Get in the house."

"Like you never drink, right?"

"Get in the house. Now!"

"You know what you are, Dad, you're a hypocrite. A hypocrite and an S.O.B."

Walking past, he muttered, "I can see why mom left you."

Reaching him in three strides, Shane grabbed him and whirled him around. "What did you say?"

Knowing she was overstepping, but unable to stop herself, Emma took his arm. "Shane, m-maybe you should go and cool off."

He paused a beat, still glaring at his son.

"Anyone could see that you're really upset. Why not go and c-cool off before this gets any uglier?"

"He doesn't need coddling, Emma, he needs consequences. He could have killed someone."

"I know that, but l-listen, the band's finishing up. Why don't you go back and see to things. I'll keep my eye on Mick until you can get away." Without waiting for an answer, she grabbed Mick's arm and propelled him toward the house.

In the living room, Mick stumbled to the couch and Emma sank into a chair beside him. "Mick, what were you thinking?"

"I dunno, let's see. Oh yeah, I was thinking that I don't care any more. About anything."

"This won't turn out good, you know that. What could be so bad that you'd take a chance on—"

"My girlfriend dumped me," he said, voice cracking. "She dumped me because she likes to go out and have a good time and he never lets me go anywhere."

"I'm sorry. I know it hurts, but—"

"Oh you know, do you?" he said, fighting tears. "Like you ever got dumped in your life."

"I got rejected all the time."

He sprawled out on the couch and closed his eyes. "That's pretty hard to believe, Miss Emma. But thanks for trying to make me feel better. "

"It's true."

"Sure it is."

"It really is. There was this one boy, his name was F-freddie and I was crazy over him."

"Freddie, huh?" he said, not opening his eyes.

"I was about your age, maybe a little older. Our school was having a spring dance. When Freddie called and invited me I was over the moon. I bought a new dress, even had my hair highlighted. I sat by the front door all night, and guess what? F-freddie never came to pick me up. Turned out it was a joke. Some sort of dare. I wanted to die, but you know what?"

No answer.

"Mick?" She nudged him with her foot and he murmured. She walked to his side and peered down into his face. Fast asleep. So much for baring her soul. "Good night, Mick," she whispered.

Covering him with a blanket, she slipped quietly out the door.

Chapter Ten

The next morning Emma was high on a ladder in the rec hall, taking down the party decorations and thinking about all of the things she wished she could have said to Mick the night before, when the door opened and Shane walked in.

"Hey, Lady. This is supposed to be your day off." The dark circles beneath his eyes belied his smile, telling her it had been a rough night.

"I got up early so I thought I'd come and help." Bracing herself against the ladder, she reached across and pulled down a handful of streamers.

"Be careful up there," he cautioned.

Emma smiled. "I will."

"I was going to have Mick do that later. If he ever gets up," he grumbled, flipping the banquet table on its side and folding down the legs.

"How did it go last night?" she asked.

"From bad to worse."

"Uh-oh."

"What it comes down to is that except for school he's not going to leave the campground for a month. And I may not let him drive again until he's forty. So now I get to be the big, bad dad again."

"M-hmm."

He propped the table against the wall and started folding down the chairs. "Do you think I'm being too rough on him?"

"Given the circumstances, no, not really." She yanked down the last of the streamers, climbed down the ladder, and deposited them in the trash can.

"It should be a pretty quiet day around here today. I'm sure Mick won't be the only one recuperating from last night."

She smiled. "I'm sure."

"I've got to run into to town later and get a new headlight at the parts store and then I'm going to try and pick out some annuals for the campground."

"Sounds like fun."

"Not really. Blair used to take care of all that. I'm pretty clueless when it comes to that sort of thing." He hesitated. "Would you like to ride along? Maybe between two of us we can figure something out."

•

An hour later as she and Shane drove into town, Emma sat in the passenger seat enjoying the scenery and the soft rock music on the radio. She chanced a glance at his profile as he drove and thought what a good man he was. It had to be difficult raising a teenager all alone and though she didn't agree with some of his decisions she gave him all the credit in the world for doing what he thought was right. She thought about the things Mick told her the day before and vowed to find a way to talk to Shane about them before the day was through.

On Adsit Street, he pulled into the auto parts store and went inside, leaving the radio playing. Emma settled back in the seat, singing along with an old Carly Simon tune and enjoying the mild breeze that blew through the open window. The Carly Simon song ended and a woman with a velvet voice began to croon about letting go and moving on with her life. She made it sound easy, and Emma wondered if she would ever be able to let go of the past and move on.

Fifteen minutes later Shane returned and stowed the headlight behind the seat. "I have an account at Gibson's Market on Hildreth Avenue. I usually get the flowers there." He slid into the driver's seat and nudged the truck into reverse. "Put your thinking cap on, Miss Emma. We'll need about thirty flats."

"Thirty? Are you s-serious?"

"We've got a lot of space to cover, sister."

As she turned the information over in her mind a thought occurred to her and she blurted, "Actually, Shane, I have an idea."

"I'm wide open to suggestions," he said with a grin.

"There's a little park off of Williams Street I go to sometimes. It has the most beautiful flower beds. Maybe we could stop there first and get some ideas."

"Works for me."

She gave him directions and he pulled onto the boulevard into the early morning traffic. Watching the familiar landmarks pass, Emma still couldn't believe she'd suggested a visit to Williams Street park. Talk about moving on. She and Beck had discovered the little hideaway shortly after moving to the city. With its fountains and foot paths and shady trees it had soon become one of their favorite retreats, a place where they shared picnics on lazy summer afternoons and crisp, leaf-strewn walks in the fall. She felt a stab of pain as they drove through the iron gates and wondered what had made her think she could handle being there with another man.

•

"Are you all right, Emma?"

"I'm fine. Why do you ask?"

"You look a little bit lost all of a sudden."

She smiled, but it wasn't quite convincing and Shane could only wonder at the secrets that lay hidden behind her beautiful gray eyes.

"There's a little walkway right around the first bend. I think that would be a good p-place to start," she said, climbing out of the truck.

A sense of peace enveloped Shane the moment they entered the park. Birds called to one another from shady trees as a gentle breeze propelled them along the cobbled path. With her full, luscious lips and the sun playing off her hair, Emma looked as beautiful and as exquisite as the daylilies that lined the trails. He shoved his hands in his pockets, nearly overwhelmed by the desire to take her hand.

"Here it is, right here." She stopped in front of a picket fence where a thick blanket of daylilies in warm yellows and deep reds flourished in the shade of a maple tree.

"Wow," he said. "Think we could recreate that bed by the sign out front?"

"We can try," she said.

"Have you got any paper in your bag?"

She dug in her purse and retrieved a small notepad and pen, handing them to him with a raised eyebrow.

Flipping to the first page, he quickly sketched the fence and the flowers, making a note of their colors while Emma peered over his shoulder.

"That's amazing."

"Not really."

"Yeah, really. I didn't know you could draw."

"In a former life I wanted to be an artist." He grinned. "Actually, I wanted to illustrate comic books. I was about fifteen at the time."

"Really?"

"I even sent away for one of those aptitude tests you used to see advertised in the backs of magazines. Scored pretty well, too."

"Why didn't you pursue your art?"

He shrugged. "Life got in the way."

They continued down the path, stopping to admire a flaming bed of orange and yellow coreopsis, a rock wall edged by a carpet of whisper soft phlox. By the time they exited the park the notebook was filled with sketches and Shane's head was filled with thoughts he knew would be better left alone; thoughts of he and Emma planting flowers together, putting down roots, building a life. But all of those things took two willing partners and she obviously wasn't interested in him as anything other than an employer. Not yet, anyway.

"Now you're the one who looks far away," she commented, as they climbed back into the truck.

"I'm not far away," he said, gazing into her beautiful gray eyes. *I'm right here, waiting. Will you ever be willing to take a chance on me, sweet Emma?*

As if hearing his thoughts, she turned away and looked out the window. After a short drive they pulled into the parking lot of the nursery, armed with sketches and determination. Emma's enthusiasm and childlike joy in the flowers was contagious and Shane felt the stress of the night before begin to ease. An hour later they emerged with flats of every flower they'd seen at the park and even some they hadn't.

"We'll fit them in somewhere," he said of the delicate columbine and the exotic lady fern that took Emma's eye.

"I can't believe we bought so many. Forty-three flats," Emma said, as they loaded them in the back of the truck.

"It seems like a lot, doesn't it?"

"It is a lot. They take up the whole back of the truck. Just wait until we get them home. I'm putting you in charge of planting them."

"Me?" she said, her pretty mouth agape. "Why not you?"

"Because I'm the boss," he said with a wink. "I get to delegate."

On impulse, he reached across and ruffled her hair. She made a grab for his hand, and he caught both of her wrists up in his. Her skin was warm and soft and his body reacted with an explosion of desire that nearly knocked the breath from his lungs. Their eyes locked for a moment before he released her.

"Want to grab some lunch before heading back?" he asked, regaining his composure.

"Sure." She looked away too quickly and he knew that she, too, had felt the fire that burned between them.

"What are you hungry for?"

"Pizza."

"Pizza it is."

Two blocks from the nursery he steered into the parking lot of Chubby's Pizzeria. Stepping inside, they saw that the restaurant was filled to overflowing with raucous children.

"They must be having a birthday party today," he commented.

A waitress appeared and seated them at a table beside the window. They perused their menus to the sounds of shrieking children.

"I haven't been here in a long time," Shane commented. "This was Mick's favorite place in the world when he was small. Blair and I used to bring him most every Saturday night."

"Would you rather eat somewhere else?" she asked.

He glanced up from his menu. "You mean because Blair and I used to come here?"

"Yeah."

"It doesn't bother me, Emma."

The waitress returned with a pitcher of water and Shane ordered a large pepperoni pizza for he and Emma, and small pizza with extra cheese and black olives to take home to Mick.

"Is she still in the area?" Emma asked, sipping her water.

"She took off for Florida the day the divorce became final. Last I knew she was working at Disney World. It's pretty symbolic, if you think about it," he said, a note of bitterness creeping into his voice. "She ran off to Disney to try and recapture the childhood I supposedly stole from her."

"Is that what she said?"

"Not in so many words, but that was the gist of it." He picked up his water glass and set it down again, making interlocking water circles on the table top. "You marry someone and you think you've got your life all mapped out. Then they decide to change the plan halfway through the trip." He erased the circles with his hand.

"I'm sure it was pretty devastating," she said softly.

"I'll survive." He took a swallow of water. "But I'm not so sure about Mick. I honestly thought he'd be better off once she split. Our house kind of turned into a war zone toward the end."

She drew in a breath and slowly let it out. "Mick thinks you blame him for the divorce."

"Did he say that?"

"Uh-huh."

He sighed as a heavy feeling settled over him. "I never wanted him to feel that way. I thought at fifteen he was old enough to understand. It was a whole lot more about me than it ever was him."

"I think all kids blame themselves on some level when their parents divorce," she said. "No matter how old they are."

"Mick's at a tough age. The Mohawk and the lip ring ... He's searching for his identity. This whole thing has kind of left him floundering. And he's not the only one." He met her gaze and held it for a long moment. "I want to apologize for the other night, Emma. It was wrong of me to presume that you'd—that we could ..." His voice trailed away and she covered his hand with hers, saving him the embarrassment of finishing.

"It's not that I didn't w-want you to stay, Shane. I'm just not ready for that kind of involvement right now."

His gaze held hers for another eternity. *And when will you be ready, Emma?* "Understood," he said, giving her hand a squeeze.

When she'd helped Shane unload the last flat of flowers from the truck, Emma stood back and stretched her arms. Her eyes skimmed across the parking lot, noticing for the first time that her parking spot was empty. She peered at the empty slot, as if that would somehow make her car reappear.

"What are you looking at?" Shane asked, following her gaze.

"It's what I'm not looking at, Shane. My car's gone."

He stared at the empty spot, his expression changing as the

realization slowly dawned. "He wouldn't."

He turned and hurried in the direction of the cabin with Emma following. A quick check of the house confirmed that Mick was nowhere inside.

"Maybe he l-left a note. I'll go and check the cottage." She hurried down the path, her pulse galloping. Please, Mick. Don't do anything stupid. Letting herself in the front door, her glance shot to the empty hook where her car keys had hung that morning. A note was propped up on the table and she grabbed it up, her heart nearly stopping as she read the scrawled message: Emma, I'm sorry for this.

"Oh, Mick ..." Stuffing the letter in her pocket, she hurried back to the cabin.

Inside, Shane eyed her expectantly.

"Looks like Mick t-took my car. I found this."

He reached for the note, barely having time to glance at it before the phone rang. Switching gears, he picked it up. "Yeah? Dusty, is that you? Slow down, I can hardly ..." His face drained of color and Emma felt her heart constrict. "Are you absolutely sure it's Mick? Alright, call the police and in the meantime stay as close as you can. I'm on my way."

As he hung up the phone, Emma noticed his hands trembling.

"Wh-what is it?"

"That was Dusty. Mick's got himself holed up in an abandoned warehouse down by the homeless shelter." His voice cracked. "He says he's pretty sure Mick's got a gun."

Chapter Eleven

Shock set in, making Shane feel like he was moving in slow motion, though a glance at the speedometer told him he was doing close to seventy. Coming up on a dangerous curve, he eased off the gas. He watched the needle on the speedometer drop to fifty and he wished he could somehow throw the brake that would stop his racing thoughts.

Dusty's call had instantly transported him back in time to the most terrifying day of his life—the afternoon when Mick, at age three, had gotten lost at the zoo. He'd taken him as a special treat for his birthday, an early attempt at father/son bonding. Up until that moment it had been one of the loveliest days of Shane's life; he and his boy enjoying the elephants and the tigers, laughing at the monkeys who performed acrobatics for them in their trees. They'd stuffed themselves with hot dogs and ice cream, and ridden the trolley car through a fantasy safari land three times.

On their way out of the park, Mick had teased for a balloon. Shane had only taken his eyes off his son for the moment it took to dig out his wallet and pay the vendor, and in that crucial moment his entire life fell apart. After a frantic forty minutes of searching, he found Mick in the aquarium, watching the manatees play in their watery world, blissfully unaware of the havoc he'd wrought. Out of his mind with worry, Shane had bargained with God, made impassioned promises to be a better, more attentive father. Feeling that same terror and helplessness now, he lifted pleading eyes to the sky and wondered whether God would give him a second chance.

•

Emma's white-knuckled grip on the arm rest had little to do with the breakneck speed at which the truck was moving. Shane's expression was grim, his eyes mirroring the trepidation she felt. She would have given anything to be able to reassure him but she was mute, paralyzed by the fear that clawed at her own insides. She'd felt it once before, the gut-twisting terror, the absolute anguish of knowing a life hung in the balance and that she was utterly helpless to save it.

The nightmares were less frequent now, but when they came, they came with shattering clarity. First, the knowing, and then the red door, growing ever farther away as she raced toward it. Her hands beating on the glass, her shrill voice screaming Beck's name, over and over, until she was too hoarse to scream any more. And finally there was the absolute darkness that came with knowing beyond a shadow of hope that she was too late. Beck was already gone.

They pulled into the alley beside the warehouse to find the cops already on the scene. Two patrol cars sat nose-to-nose at the entrance, lights strobing. Beside them, Dusty stood talking to two uniformed officers. As Shane and Emma climbed out of the truck, one of the officers hurried over.

"You the boy's father?"

"Yeah."

"Okay, good." Turning, he motioned to the other officer. "Callahan?"

The other cop walked over and extended his hand. "Joe Callahan."

"Shane Lucy."

"Mr. Lucy, can you tell me what's going on with your son?"

"We had an argument last night. He'd been drinking." Shane ran a trembling hand through his hair. "I didn't think I was that hard on him, to make him resort to this."

He indicated Dusty. "That homeless man over there says the boy's got a gun."

Shane sucked in a breath. "One of my hunting rifles is missing from the gun safe."

The cop made a note in his pad. "What sort of rifle is it?"

"It's a thirty-thirty."

He let out a low whistle. "How much ammo has he got?"

"I don't know."

After asking what seemed a million questions he flipped his notepad shut. "We've got a crisis counselor on the way. Deb Swink's the best there is, but it's going to be awhile before she can get here. Your son won't let us anywhere near him, but I've got a radio set up at the warehouse entrance so we can hear what's going on. Would you like to try and talk to him?"

"Of course."

The two men strode toward the warehouse with Emma following. Stopping at the entrance, Callahan called, "Mick, how are you doing in there, buddy?"

After a heart stopping pause, Mick's voice came back through the radio. "Just go away and leave me alone."

"We want to help you try and work through this, Mick. I've got your dad out here. He'd like to come in and talk to you, if that's alright."

"Get him out of here!" Mick shouted. "I don't want to see him."

Seeing Shane's anguish, Emma laid a gentle hand on his shoulder. "It'll b-be alright," she said, hoping to God it was true. The officer seemed to notice her for the first time.

"Are you a relative?"

"No, just a f-friend."

"Are you close to Mick?"

"I haven't known him very long, but we t-talk sometimes."

"Do you think he'd talk to you now?"

"I don't kn-know."

"What's your name?"

"Emma Beckman."

Turning, he called back into the warehouse. "How about Emma, Mick? Would you talk to Emma for a little while?"

Time seemed to slow and then stop completely. Beads of sweat broke out on Emma's forehead as she waited until finally, Mick's voice came back through the radio. "Yeah, I'll talk to Emma."

Shane grabbed her hand and gave it a squeeze.

"Alright, that's a good sign," Callahan said. "Just try to keep him talking until Deb gets here."

"I'll do my b-best," she said. And then, with a deep breath for courage and a whispered prayer for wisdom, Emma stepped inside the warehouse.

Walking through darkness, she scanned the shadows, stopping for a moment to let her eyes adjust before continuing on. Her footsteps echoed on the hard packed floor, keeping a rhythm with every beat of her heart. Shivering with cold and apprehension, she paused before an open doorway.

"Mick?" she called softly.

"I'm over here."

Turning, she peered into the shadows. Mick sat huddled against a wall, looking small and scared, a shotgun cradled in his hands.

"Wh-what's going on, Mick?"

"I'm giving up, Emma," he said, his voice choked with tears. "I just don't care anymore. About anything."

She took a step closer. "Sounds like you're pretty discouraged."

He let out a short, humorless bark of laughter. "Yeah, I guess you could say that."

"C-can you tell me what happened?"

"My girlfriend is pregnant."

Emma took another breath before sliding to the floor, twenty feet from where he sat. "That's hard. But it's not the end of the world, is it? I mean, you have options. If you don't feel ready to be a father you can always give the baby up for adoption."

"I don't have crap for options, Emma. The baby's not mine. I never touched her."

Emma shifted gears as she digested this new piece of information. "I see."

"I never touched her and now she's pregnant. She said she loved me. Does that sound like love to you?" His shoulders shook with sobs and Emma ached to pull him in her arms and comfort him.

"Listen, Mick, I know you probably don't want to hear this right now, but some day you're going to meet a sp-special girl. One who deserves your love, I promise you will."

"They're all the same," he said angrily. "A bunch of liars, just like my mother. None of them do what they say they will, and I'm damn sick and tired of promises that never come true."

Emma searched her mind for a suitable response. Before she could formulate one, Mick said softly, "I'm tired of waiting to be picked up for the dance."

"What?"

"It's just like what you said about that guy, Freddie. How he left you by the window, waiting for him to come and take you to the dance. And it was all a big joke." He wiped his eyes on his sleeve. "Just before my mom left she promised she was going to come back for me when she got settled in Florida. She was going to have me come and live with her, get me free passes to DisneyWorld any time I wanted them. I waited a whole year, waiting for a phone call or a letter, and it was nothing but a load of crap." Pain oozed from his every word, bringing tears to Emma's eyes.

"And let's not even talk about my dad. Mom left because she didn't want to be tied down to a kid anymore, and now my father hates me for it."

"That's n-not true. Your father loves you very much."

"It doesn't matter now anyway." He clutched the rifle. "It all ends right here. I'll be doing them both a favor."

"Is that what you think?" Anger rose up inside her, mingling with sorrow and fear. "B-because you're dead wrong. What you'd be doing is sentencing everyone who cares about you to a life of guilt and sadness and nightmares that will never go away."

"You don't know that."

"Yes, Mick. I do know it."

He sniffled. "How?"

"Because my husband took his life."

"I thought you told my dad he had an accident."

"He did."

"Well if it was an accident, then …"

The trembling started from deep inside as the memories tore through her like a hurricane, tearing open wounds that hadn't begun to heal. Everything inside her fought against them, but knowing it might be her only chance to save this brokenhearted boy, she braced herself against the fear and sorrow and let the words come out.

"I wasn't so much older than you when I met Beck. But the first minute I saw him, I knew he was the only one for me. I d-didn't think anyone could ever love me. I d-didn't believe him when he said he did. I kept waiting for it to fall apart, but the feelings got stronger with every day, every minute we spent together we were more in love. After a couple of years we got married and bought a house. We were going to fix it up just the way we wanted it and then we were going to fill it with kids." Her voice broke and she paused to regain control.

"So what happened?" Mick asked.

"Beck worked for an industrial contracting company in the city.

They got a bid to overhaul a big old hotel out on Brewster Street. It was a dangerous job, but Beck said the m-money would put us over the edge. We'd be able to finally finish the house, and be comfortable enough to start a family." She swallowed. "But it didn't happen that way."

"Why not?"

"The third day on the job part of the old roof caved in. Beck fell to the ground and b-broke his back. The s-surgeon did all he could, but they told us Beck would never be able to work again. He'd never walk without canes, and probably never have children."

"Oh, wow."

"My husband was a very strong man. He t-tried to keep his spirits up, but the constant pain and the disappointment were too much for him in the end. He felt like he wasn't worth anything any more. But he was worth the world to me."

Tears streamed, unchecked, down her face. "One morning, about a year after the accident, I w-went out with a friend for the day. I never did that after the accident. I never wanted to leave him alone, but my friend was in town from Philly that day so Beck insisted. Dove and I went shopping, and then we stopped for lunch. We were talking like girlfriends do, shooting the breeze, and then Dove g-got this terrible look on her face. 'Emma,' she said, 'You have to go home right now.' I got a terrible feeling in my stomach because Dove knew things, sensed things. She could see th-things other people couldn't. I hurried back home, but by the time I got there it was t-too late." She closed her eyes, reliving the nightmare.

After a long silence, Mick said softly, "Too late for what?"

"After I left that morning Beck locked himself in the garage. He started up his truck, then he laid d-down on the floor beside the exhaust pipe and he went to sleep. F-forever."

"Oh, Em."

"I t-torture myself with if only's. If only I hadn't left him alone that day. If only we'd tried one more surgeon, one more therapist. But none of that really matters, because what it comes down to in the end is that my l-love wasn't enough to live for." She added softly, "I wasn't enough."

The words were torture. Her battered heart begged her to stop their flow, all the while, knowing she couldn't.

"We c-could never have had the life we dreamed of before the accident, but we could have had something. Now all I have is an empty hole where my husband should be. But he never will be again." She wiped away her tears with her hands. "He thought he was doing what was b-best for me, but suicide is never the best thing, Mick. It's never the right choice. Not for the ones who are left behind." Through the dusky shadows she saw tears glistening in Mick's eyes.

"Give me the gun, Mick. You don't really want to hurt yourself, or anyone else. Do you?"

Silence fell like a rainstorm. Knowing she'd played the only card in her deck, Emma waited, barely breathing, until at last Mick stood. He walked to her and set the rifle at her feet. "I'm sorry, Emma," he said. "For everything."

She stood and held out her arms. Mick fell into them, sobbing. "I know, s-sweetheart," she said, stroking his hair. "Life's hard right now. But it'll get better. I promise." She held him, prayers of thanks screaming in her head, until he stopped crying. And then, hand in hand, they stepped back out into the daylight.

Outside, Emma saw that a small crowd had gathered. Dusty stood on the fringes, his face breaking into a grin when Mick emerged. A half dozen more officers had joined the first two. Emma scanned the crowd, searching for Shane. He stood off to the side, speaking softly with a small woman who had the kindest eyes Emma had ever seen. When Mick appeared they fell silent, Shane watching his son with more raw emotion on his face than Emma had ever seen. And then he was at their side.

"I'm sorry, Dad," Mick choked. "I didn't mean to hurt anyone."

His words were swallowed up as Shane wrapped him in a hug. Emma watched as they held each other, sending up another prayer that both father and son would survive the long, hard journey ahead.

"You did a stellar job in there, Emma." She turned to see Joe Callahan looking at her with open admiration. "Deb thinks we should sign you on as a counselor."

"I'm just g-glad I could help."

"We're going to have to take him over to the hospital for a psych evaluation. He won't want to go, they never do. Maybe you could break it to him?"

"Alright."

Seeing the excitement was over, the crowd slowly drifted away. Once again drawing on an inner strength she hadn't known she possessed, Emma laid her hand on Mick's arm. "Mick, they want to t-take you over to the hospital now and have you checked out."

"For what?"

"A psychiatrist will want to talk to you."

Realization dawned in his eyes, and on the heels of it, fear. "Will you come with me?"

"Of course I will."

Shane followed in his truck as Emma and Mick rode to the hospital in the back of a patrol car. Mick's knees were shaking, his hand gripping hers. "Are they gonna lock me up, ya think?"

"They just want to talk to you, Mick, help you sort things out."

They reached the hospital within minutes and Emma stayed with Mick until a psychiatric aide came and led him away. She watched until the double doors of the psych ward swallowed him up. When they locked behind him, she slumped against the wall, feeling completely drained.

Shane appeared and stood before her, and she lifted her gaze to meet his. "How are you holding up?" he asked.

"I'm alright. How about you?"

He blew out a breath. "I'm hanging in there. They're going to admit him. I gave them all his information. I guess there's nothing we can do now except wait."

"Then that's what we d-do."

"Think there's any place around here to get a cup of coffee?"

They found the hospital cafeteria, bought two cups of strong, black coffee, and carried them back to the waiting room, where a nurse informed them the doctor would see them as soon as possible.

Shane took a swallow of coffee. "I don't know what I would have done without you today, Emma. You saved my son's life. Thank you doesn't begin to cover that."

"There's no need to thank me, Shane. I know I haven't known him very long, but Mick's become very special to me. I'm so glad I could help."

He was quiet for a moment. "I'm sorry about what you went through with Beck. I had no idea."

Her eyes shot to his face. "You heard that?"

"I heard every word you said, Emma. I know it couldn't have been easy for you, reliving that experience."

She dropped her gaze and his hand slid to hers, enveloping it. They sat without speaking, the moments ticking away into hours, until finally the doctor appeared.

"Mr. Lucy?"

Shane stood and shook his hand. "How is he?"

"I'd say pretty well, all things considered. Please, sit."

When they were seated the doctor continued. "Your son suffers from severe depression. He recently found out his girlfriend is pregnant with someone else's child, and he also says his mother left. Is that true?"

"About a year ago."

"He's having an extremely difficult time adjusting to that. This episode was a definite cry for help."

"Do you think he'll try it again?"

"It's hard to say for sure, but since his depression appears to be situational rather than pathological I think he's got an excellent chance of getting well. He'll need a lot of patience and support, but I think he'll get through it. We'll set you up with a family therapist for group counseling sessions if you're agreeable to that."

"I'll do whatever it takes."

The doctor smiled. "That's half the battle, my friend."

"Can I see him?"

The doctor paused. "He doesn't want to see you right now, Mr. Lucy. He's embarrassed and angry and about a dozen other things, too. We'll give him a mild sedative to make sure he gets a good night's sleep. And then we'll go from there."

•

By the time they returned home, the campground was enveloped in darkness. "It seems like a hundred years ago since we left," Shane said.

"It's been quite a day."

He cut the engine and they climbed out of the truck.

"Feel like dinner?" he asked.

"My stomach's still a mess," she confessed. "I don't think I could eat a thing."

"How about a drink, then?"

Sensing his invitation stemmed from a need for a listening ear,

Emma smiled. "I think I know just the one."

While Shane went to the office to check his messages, Emma got busy in the kitchen. Warming a pan of milk on the stove, she rummaged in the cupboard for cinnamon and nutmeg. When Shane returned, she handed him a foaming mug.

He took a swallow. "What do you call this?"

"Sweet milk. I had a friend once whose grandmother used to make it for us after a bad day."

"Well, I'd say this day certainly qualifies."

"Mmm."

She followed him to the living room and sat down on the couch beside him. Seeing he was struggling with his emotions, she remained quiet, giving him time to sort himself out.

"I've been holding on too tightly because I didn't want to lose him. And I almost lost him anyway." Tears gathered on his lashes and he buried his face in his hands. "I never would have forgiven myself if he'd …"

"Shane, listen to me." She laid a gentle hand on his back. "This is not your fault. It's not easy raising kids, especially these days. Everything's more complicated than it used to be. You're doing the b-best you can. I know it, and deep down, so does Mick."

"Do you really think so?"

"I know so."

She removed her hand and he caught it up in his and lightly kissed her fingers. "Thanks."

They talked for the better part of an hour, until Emma's eyelids started to droop. "It's getting late," she said. "We should both get some sleep. We'll need to be rested for tomorrow."

"Would you stay here tonight, Emma? I mean, in the guest room?"

"Sure."

Moments later she pulled back the blankets, crawled under the multicolored quilt, and crashed into sleep.

She awoke what seemed moments later to the insistent ringing of the telephone. Opening her eyes, she was surprised to see daylight filtering through the curtains. A glance at the bedside clock told her it was nearly ten o'clock. She padded to the kitchen where Shane already had a pot of coffee brewing. He stood with his back to her, talking on the phone.

"Alright. I'll be there shortly." Replacing it in the cradle, he met Emma's questioning gaze. "That was the hospital. Mick's ready to see me now."

Chapter Twelve

After a quick breakfast and a change of clothes, Shane was ready to roll. Stepping out the front door, he felt a heaviness in the air and saw that the sky was dark with rain clouds.

The overcast weather mirrored his uneasy feeling, punctuating the knots of dread that tightened in his stomach at the thought of seeing Mick, as if he were going to visit a hostile alien and not a beloved son. The questions that had tortured him in the night now swirled in his brain like debris swirling in a hurricane, demanding answers he couldn't begin to give. Where had he gone wrong as a parent? How had he allowed himself to become such a miserable failure that his son had to resort to a suicide attempt in order to get his attention?

"Give Mick a hug for me," Emma said, breaking into his thoughts.

"Will do." He glanced at the sky and then back into her eyes. "Things should be pretty quiet around here today. Looks like we've got a storm coming, so people will probably clear out pretty fast."

"Don't worry about a thing here. Everything will be fine."

Her confidence was contagious and he felt the knots in his stomach loosen. "Alex should be here any time now," he said. "He knows what he has to do. Give him a shout if anything comes up. He's basically a pretty responsible kid."

"Alright."

"Alright then, I'll see you when I get back." Pausing, he added, "Maybe we can have dinner together."

"I'd like that." She gave his hand a squeeze, adding softly, "Good luck today."

Her smile was warm and genuine, and it gave him the courage to face what lay ahead.

When Shane's truck pulled from the lot, Emma returned to her cottage to change into a clean pair of jeans and T-shirt. She tidied her hair and applied a coat of concealer to the dark circles beneath her eyes before heading back to the store. She was more than an hour late, but true to Shane's prediction, the campground was quiet that morning.

She made a fresh pot of coffee and was stocking the newspaper racks with the morning's edition of the Daily Gazette when the door opened and Dusty walked in.

"Good morning, Dusty," she said, doing her best to hide her surprise. Gone was the brash, obnoxious creature she'd met four days earlier. The man who stood before her was humble and ill at ease and not in the least unattractive. His eyes were clear and blue and he'd taken pains to shave and wash his hair.

"Morning, Emma," he said, eyes cast downward as he fidgeted with the change in his pockets. "Thought I'd come by and see how Mick made out last night."

"They kept him at the hospital overnight. Shane's on his way there now."

"I figured as much." He lifted his eyes to meet hers. "Is there anything I can do to help out around here?"

The offer was made with sincerity and Emma didn't have the heart to turn him away. "I'll bet Alex could use a hand," she said, reaching for her two-way radio. "He'll have both his work and Mick's to do today."

She radioed Alex, asking him to report to the store and pick Dusty up, then poured Dusty a cup of coffee. Accepting it from her hands, he took a swallow.

"About the other day," he said, shifting uncomfortably in his shoes. "I'm sorry I acted like such a jerk. I had no right to talk to you that way."

She waved his words away. "Forget about it."

Moments later Alex pulled up in the golf cart. As Dusty turned to leave, Emma touched his arm. "I'm awfully glad you were there yesterday, Dusty. I hate to think what might have happened if you hadn't called us."

Gratitude flickered in his eyes and in that moment Emma felt the fragile seeds of friendship begin to grow between them.

•

As he stepped off the elevator and onto the fifth floor psychiatric ward at Sisters of Mercy Hospital, Shane's breakfast rolled over in his stomach. Pushing out a breath, he walked toward a set of locked double doors where a sign instructed: ring bell for assistance.

He dutifully pushed the button and waited until a brusque female voice answered. "Yes?"

"I'm here to see my son, Mick Lucy."

Hearing the click of the locks, he pulled open the door and stepped into a cold, slightly sour smelling hallway. His eyes flicked over the pale green walls, taking in brightly colored posters bearing the idioms, *Today is Beautiful*, *One Day at a Time*, and *You Are Special*.

At the end of the hallway two nurses sat at a desk behind a thick glass window. Lifting her hand, the larger of the two motioned him closer and slid the window open a crack. "Mick's probably in the activities room. Second door on the left," she told him.

An angry looking young man glared at him from a chair beside the nurses station, while another man shuffled past, mumbling obscenities. Averting his gaze, Shane walked past them and opened the door.

The activities room was painted the same drab green color as the hallway with the same kinds of posters littering the walls. In the center of the room a large television set played reruns of I Love Lucy for no one. Mick sat in the corner, looking out the window at the rain. He was the picture of dejection and Shane's heart stirred inside him. He took a hesitant step forward.

"Hey, Mick."

"Hey," Mick said, not turning from the window.

Shane took another step and slid into the chair across from him. "How are you?"

Mick shrugged. "There aren't any doctors here today because of the holiday. They say I have to stay until Wednesday. I'm here to tell you, this place sucks."

"I know. But it's only for a couple of days. Just until we can be sure you're okay." His voice caught and he swallowed the lump that formed in his throat.

"I'm okay."

"I hope so."

Shane sat in silence, watching the rain. He heard raucous

laughter blaring from the TV and wondered whether he'd ever have a reason to laugh again.

"It's just … I get tired of feeling like a loser, ya know?"

"I'm sorry if I let you down. If I made you feel that you couldn't talk to me," Shane said, reciting the words he'd spent most of the night preparing. "If I somehow made you feel like you were to blame for the divorce, because you weren't."

Mick nodded.

"I want you to know that no matter what, I'm proud to be your dad," Shane continued, pushing out the words that screamed for release in his heart and in his head. "I guess I don't show it enough, but I love you, Mick. More than you could ever imagine."

Tears fell from Mick's eyes and he scrubbed at them with the back of his hand. "I'm really sorry, Dad," he said, choking on his tears. "I guess I screwed up big time."

"I guess we both did, kid." As he pulled Mick into his embrace, he felt the black cloud of despair begin to roll away, replaced by a glimmer of hope for brighter days ahead.

◆

Throughout the day Emma's thoughts turned to Shane more times than she could count. He was never far from her mind and as she restocked displays and tidied the storage room she found herself sending out positive energy and hoping the visit was going well. She didn't want to admit even to herself how much she was looking forward to being with him at the end of the day.

By five o'clock, the drizzle had progressed to a steady downpour and all but the permanents had checked out of the campground. Emma locked up the store and dashed across the parking lot to the office. Letting herself in, she saw that the answering machine blinked with messages. Stowing the bank bag in the file cabinet, she walked to the phone and hit the play button.

After three hang-ups a woman's angry voice filled the quiet of the room. "Shane, what in the hell is going on up there?" There was a pause and Emma heard her exhale a stream of cigarette smoke. "Okay, so I guess you're not there. Call me on my cell as soon as you get this message. I'll have it on twenty-four seven."

The call clicked off and the machine's mechanical voice informed her the call had been received at seven fifty-nine that morning. She made a mental note to tell Shane about it as soon as he arrived home.

The next voice that came through the machine was Shane's.

"Hey, Emma. Looks like I'm going to be here for most of the day. I'll probably be home around eight. I hope we're still on for dinner."

She thought of the unmasked pain in his eyes and of the sheer vulnerability she'd seen in him the night before and felt a stirring sensation deep inside. In those desperate hours he'd ceased being her boss and become a kindred spirit, a fellow traveler on the road of pain and sorrow. She felt closer to Shane Lucy in that moment than any human being on the face of the Earth.

Letting herself in the cabin's private entrance, she made her way down the hall to the kitchen. Rummaging in the cupboards, she found a canister of corn meal, two cans of crushed tomatoes, and one of kidney beans. Considering the damp, dreary day, chili and cornbread seemed a perfect choice, so she rolled up her sleeves and went to work. Twenty minutes later, with the chili simmering on the stove, she put the corn bread in the oven and headed back to her cottage to freshen up.

•

Shane pulled from the hospital parking lot in a much brighter frame of mind than he'd entered it that morning. He thought back over the day. All things considered, it had gone alright. He and Mick had communicated more in the past ten hours than they had in a year. And though he knew it would take more than a day to restore their relationship, the prospect didn't seem as daunting as it had the day before. Baby steps, he thought. One day at a time, just like the posters said.

A subtle frown tugged at the corners of his mouth. On Wednesday Mick would be coming home and they would begin to rebuild their lives. He thought of Emma and the calming influence she was on them both, and was amazed at how entrenched she'd become in their hearts in such a short amount of time. And though he had no right to, he hoped she would want to continue to be a part of it.

As a friend, he told himself. But even as his mind formed the words, he knew his feelings went much deeper than that. The confession she'd made to Mick in the warehouse had only served to strengthen the fierce protectiveness he felt for her. He wanted so badly to pull her into his arms and into his heart and take all her sadness away. If only she'd let him.

The feeling was reinforced a half hour later when he pulled into the parking lot at the campground and saw soft lights glowing in the windows of the cabin. A pang of desire shot through him; not just a physical need, but an emotional one. A need for companionship and comfort, for a connection with someone.

No, not just someone, he thought. *Emma.*

Moving closer, he peered in the window. She stood at the stove preparing dinner, a hint of a smile lighting her angel face. The sight warmed him through. He'd stopped at a Chinese restaurant on the way home and picked up dinner but he liked Emma's idea a lot better. Walking to the garbage can, he opened the lid and dumped the carry-out boxes inside.

•

"Something sure smells good in here."

At the sound of Shane's voice a small thrill went through Emma's heart and she turned to him with a smile. "I didn't have a lot to work with, so it's potluck. How did it go today?"

"So far, so good," he said, removing his rain-soaked jacket. "They recommended a couple of counselors in town, so I'll have to see about getting set up for some sessions next week. What can I do to help you here?"

"There's a salad in the fridge, if you want to grab it. I think everything else is ready."

As Shane retrieved the salad bowl, Emma carried the pot of chili and the corn bread to the table. Her gaze moved over his damp hair and beard-stubbled chin and her insides stirred again.

"Mick seemed okay, then?"

"Better than I expected. We talked a lot, but I have a feeling we need to talk a whole lot more." He picked up his water glass and took a swallow. "How's everything here?"

"Quiet. Dusty stopped by this morning."

He glanced at her in surprise. "Really?"

"He wanted to help out, so I had him work with Alex today. I hope that's alright. He seems to be trying so hard."

"I'll talk to him," Shane said. "If he can stay on the straight and narrow, maybe we can work something out. After yesterday I feel I owe him the chance to try." He added softly, "I owe both of you, big time."

She looked into his eyes and saw gratitude, and something else; something mysterious and filled with yearning that both thrilled and terrified her.

"M-maybe we could put Dusty in charge of planting the flower beds," she said, steering the conversation into safer waters.

"That's a thought," he said, turning his gaze away.

The awkward moment passed and they fell into easy conversation, discussing the garden spots they'd planned and ideas for the campground's summer entertainment. When the meal was finished Shane stood and carried his dishes to the sink while Emma dumped the leftover chili into a Rubbermaid bowl.

With the food put away, she turned on the faucet and began to rinse the plates and the silverware. As Shane opened the door to fill the dishwasher his hand accidentally brushed against her thigh. A hot current of desire shot through her and she startled, losing her hold on the sprayer nozzle. It slipped from her hands, causing a stream of water to splash his shirt.

"Hey, watch what you're doing!"

"Oh gosh, I'm s-sorry." Noticing the soggy wet stain, she clapped her hand over her mouth.

"You don't look all that sorry to me," he said.

She grabbed a dish towel from the rack and swiped at the water stain, making it worse.

"Oh yeah, that's much better," he groused, causing Emma to burst into giggles.

Plucking a drinking glass from the sink, he filled it with water and threw it at her. She squealed as the icy cold liquid splashed her skin. "What are you doing?"

"There's something you should know about me, Miss Emma," he said with a sly grin. "I don't get mad, I get even."

Grabbing the hose, she turned on the water and sprayed him full in the face, yelping as he grabbed her up in his arms and tickled her without mercy. She struggled against him, laughing until she couldn't breathe. "Okay, s-stop! I give up!"

He ceased the torturous tickling, his mouth inches from hers. "You sure?"

"Yeah," she gasped. "I'm sure."

His lips drew closer still, finally touching down on hers. His kiss was fierce and hungry, and as his tongue found hers she gave in to the pleasure of it until her legs were weak and her nether regions tingling. His arms tightened around her and she felt as if she were at sea, floating away on wave after wave of pleasure. After what seemed an eternity, his lips released hers, but his eyes held her fast.

"I love you, Emma," he whispered.

Before she could react the back door banged open and a woman burst through. Her startlingly blue eyes flashed with anger and her short, blonde hair dripped with rain as she tossed an overnight bag onto the floor.

"I called you a hundred times," she said, her eyes skimming over Emma with contempt. "Now I can see why you were too busy to call me back."

Shane's arms fell away and Emma saw his face move through a series of changes: shock, disbelief, and finally, anger. He stood, glaring at the woman. When he finally spoke, his voice was the cold, hard texture of granite.

"What are you doing here, Blair?"

Chapter Thirteen

The woman's icy gaze flicked over Emma again before returning to Shane. "I got a call last night from a friend of a friend who told me my son was in the psychiatric ward at Sisters of Mercy Hospital. They seemed to think I should have that piece of information, considering I am his mother."

"I was going to call you later tonight," Shane said.

"Well, I guess I saved you the trouble, didn't I?" As she shrugged out of her jacket, her gaze returned to Emma. "Who's your friend?"

Shane's jaw tensed and Emma could see he was working hard to control his temper. "This is my assistant, Emma Beckman."

She brushed past Emma without a word of acknowledgment and threw her coat over the back of a chair. "Got any coffee? I've had a hell of a long day."

Without waiting for an answer, she removed a coffee cup from the dish drainer and poured it full. She took a swallow, stirred in a spoonful of sugar, and sat down at the kitchen table. "Now," she said, giving Shane a level stare. "Would you like to tell me what's going on with my son?"

The atmosphere in the room was as chilly as the rain and Emma felt goose bumps rise on her arms. Knowing her presence was the reason, she grabbed up her jacket.

"I should go," she told Shane.

"You don't have to leave, Emma."

"It's getting l-late and you and Blair have things to talk about."

"You'll get soaked through. At least stay until the rain lets up."

"I'll be f-fine." She hurried toward the door with Shane following. When it closed behind them, he raked his hands through his hair.

"I'm sorry, Emma. This is awkward as hell."

"It's alright."

"No, it isn't. She shouldn't have shown up here like this."

"Even so, the two of you have f-family matters to discuss. You don't need an audience."

"Anything Blair and I have to discuss can wait. I'm going to walk you back to your cottage."

"Shane, don't be silly. G-go back in and talk to her. I'll see you in the morning."

"Are you sure?"

"I'm positive." She gave him a smile and a kiss on the cheek before stepping from the porch and into the welcoming cover of darkness.

·

Blair's timing could not have been worse if she'd intentionally set out to ruin his life. Counting ten to calm himself, Shane walked back inside. Blair sat at the table, punching a text message into her cell phone. She snapped it shut when he walked in.

"So, when did you hire an assistant?" she asked, her smile belied by the sarcasm in her voice.

He folded his arms across his chest. "A few days ago."

She raised an eyebrow. "She works fast."

His anger sparked. "Excuse me, Blair, but I don't really see how that concerns you."

She laughed. "It doesn't concern me in the least. But it obviously concerns Mick plenty."

"How so?"

She let out a long-suffering sigh, as if she were explaining life to a preschooler. "Obviously the fact that you've replaced me is upsetting my son."

He stared at her in disbelief. "Mick adores Emma. In fact if she hadn't been there to talk him down last night I hate to think how things might have turned out."

"Which brings me to the point. I've had a real long drive and it gave me lots of time to think. I'm taking you back to court, Shane. I'm going to get custody of Mick."

His spark of anger ignited, racing through his veins like an inferno. "The hell you are."

"It's clearly not working out, him being here with you. I knew I should have taken him with me last year."

"But you didn't take him, did you? As usual, you thought only of yourself." He glared at her, more infuriated than he could ever remember being. He'd almost forgotten how irrational and self-centered his ex-wife could be.

"Let's try to stay calm, Shane," she said. "I can see you're letting your feelings for this woman interfere with your good judgment. Shouting and getting ugly with each other is not going to help matters."

Shane felt a migraine explode inside his head. Of all the things he disliked about his ex-wife, he hated the way she analyzed him and invalidated his feelings the most. But she was right about one thing. Mick had big problems, and his parents being at war with each other wasn't going to help solve them.

"What do you want from me, Blair?"

"For starters, I want you to tell me what happened."

He started at the beginning, telling her about Mick's guilt feelings over the divorce, about his girlfriend's pregnancy and his problems at school. "He feels like I've been too hard on him," he finally said. "I never claimed to be a perfect parent, but I'm doing the best I can. Mick and I are working through this and we'll be fine in the end. As for you getting custody, you can get that out of your head right now."

She sighed. "Maybe that was a little bit hasty of me, but I've been out of my mind with worry." She took a swallow of coffee and set her cup on the table in front of her. "But now that I'm here, I'm thinking maybe I should stay. At least for awhile."

Shane's headache spread through his body like a poison until every muscle and joint ached. Six months earlier he would have done anything in his power to hear Blair say those words. Now the very thought of them made him ill. Why was it that just when a man felt couldn't handle one more thing, life handed him one more thing?

"You don't seem very pleased with the idea," she said.

"What about your job?"

"I can take a leave of absence."

He stared at her, trying to digest the idea, to reconcile himself to the thought of having her around. He couldn't do it, couldn't even imagine such a thing.

"Look, I know that three's a crowd. I'll check into a motel

tomorrow, will that be acceptable?" she asked.

"I suppose so."

"Would you like me to sleep in my car tonight? Would that be easier for you?"

"You can sleep in the guest room for tonight," he said gruffly. "We'll sort everything else out in the morning."

With nothing left to do or say, he turned and stalked out, one thought burning in his brain. He had to find Emma, to explain. He'd meant to woo her slowly, to win her over a day and a moment at a time. Instead, he'd blurted out his feelings like a love-struck teenager. He could only imagine what she must be thinking now.

He trudged down the path to her cottage and knocked loudly on the front door. When there was no response, he peered in the windows. The house was dark and quiet. Digging in his heels, he sat on the steps to wait for her. He'd wait all night if he had to.

The rain pounded him relentlessly and within minutes he was soaked to the skin.

"What kind of fool am I?" he muttered. She was likely inside, sitting in the dark, avoiding him. He stood and trudged back up the path. He'd give her some space, then, for tonight. But tomorrow they were going to get things straight.

●

There was something about walking in the rain that Emma had always found therapeutic. The scent and feel of fresh, clean rainwater always seemed to clear her head. And if ever her thoughts were in need of clarification, it was that night. She wandered along the beach, trying to sort herself out until the distant rumble of thunder sent her scurrying back to her cottage.

She'd experienced the full spectrum of emotions that night— desire, pleasure, guilt, fear. All of them had been swallowed up in icy numbness with a look into Blair's eyes. Discovered in Shane's embrace, she felt as if she'd been caught with her hand in the cookie jar. Never mind that the jar no longer belonged to Blair.

Or did it?

She stepped onto the porch of her cottage and reached in her pocket for her key, trying not to think about the energy she'd felt swirling in the air between Shane and his ex-wife. Was it simply anger, or was it something more?

A damp chill greeted her as she opened the door and stepped

inside. Shivering, she made her way to the kitchen and warmed a glass of cinnamon milk, knowing it wouldn't stave off the cold she felt, the fear and uncertainty that hovered like a cloud above her as she wondered what was happening back at the cabin. Her mind said it was none of her business, but her heart couldn't seem to let it go. It whispered a truth she was nowhere near prepared to face. She was falling for Shane, harder and faster than she'd ever imagined possible, and the thought of losing him filled her with dread.

How had it happened so quickly?

She'd been physically attracted to him from the moment they met, despite his brusque exterior. As the days passed, she'd caught glimpses of the loving, compassionate man inside of him and her attraction had grown deeper. Tonight's kiss had confirmed the feelings she'd only just begun to let herself acknowledge. She was falling for him. No, falling was an understatement. She was crashing headlong into love. Shane had said he loved her, but Blair's return changed everything.

Leaving the milk to warm on the stove, she went into the bedroom and stripped off her wet clothes. Wrapped in a quilt, she returned to the living room and sank into a chair beside the window, watching as lightning flashed across the lake. She thought about Beck, and about the pain of letting go. She'd allowed herself to believe she could start again ... love again, but now the searing pain in her chest reinforced the truth she'd faced on the day they laid Beck in the ground. In the game of love, only the strong survived. Too emotionally fragile to weather the storms, she was destined to travel life's journey alone.

•

When the morning sun spread its crimson veil across Shadow Lake, Emma awakened in her chair, a vague headache creeping up the back of her neck. After a warm shower and a strong cup of coffee she pulled on a pair of jeans and a hoodie and went to open the store.

Lost in her thoughts, she was startled to see Dusty waiting for her on the porch, looking every bit as discomfited as she felt.

"Good morning, Dusty."

"Hello, Emma." His gaze met hers briefly before falling away. "Shane's heading back to the hospital this morning. He said I should help out in the store today."

"Alright."

He cast a glance at the cabin. "When did she get back?"

"Last night."

He blew out a breath, muttering, "I see she hasn't changed a bit."

There was a hint of bitterness beneath his words that Emma could only wonder about. Before she could question him, the door of the cabin opened and Shane appeared on the porch. Emma's heart leapt at the sight of him and she ached to rush into his arms and seek reassurance.

"Morning, Emma." His smile was warm, but there was no mistaking the weariness in his eyes.

"Good morning."

"I'm going to run back up and see Mick today. I shouldn't be too late, but Dusty's going to stick close by in case you need anything."

"Alright."

"When I get back we need to talk."

Before she could respond the door opened again and Blair stepped outside. As she crossed the parking lot Emma took in her silky red capris and matching sandals. Her hair was carefully gelled into spikes and her face was magazine cover perfect. She looked like she was competing in a fashion show and Emma felt shabby by comparison.

She walked past Emma and Dusty without a glance and climbed into Shane's truck. Emma watched, uneasiness swirling inside her as Shane climbed behind the wheel and the two of them drove away.

It wasn't until the truck disappeared down the road that Dusty broke the silence. "She's the last thing he needs around here right now."

Emma faced him in surprise. "Why do you say that?"

"She's always stirring everyone up, making things worse. She's a sneaky one. Always has been."

Emma had secretly thought that Dusty might be the 'friend of a friend' who'd tipped Blair off. Knowing they were on the same page about her, she felt the bond between them grow stronger.

"Still and all, she is Mick's mother. He needs all the support he can get right now. No matter where it comes from."

"You may be right," he said, not sounding at all convinced.

Emma's gaze wandered across the campground and came to rest on the flats of flowers she and Shane had bought. Vibrant and beautiful, the very sight of them lifted her spirits. What better way to welcome Mick home than to fill the campground with their beauty?

"I have an idea," she said, patting Dusty's arm. "Do you think between the two of us we could get these flowers planted today?"

•

Shane drove without speaking, his hands gripping the wheel, while Blair sat in the passenger seat, her fingers working furiously on the key pad of her cell phone. One more irritating habit to add to her collection, he thought. Not that she had to do anything at all. Her very presence seemed to put him on edge.

His sideways glance took in her designer clothes and perfectly manicured hands. Her meticulous attention to her appearance was one of the things he'd always loved about her. Now it annoyed him and he couldn't fathom why. His mind wandered to Emma. Beautiful Emma, with a kindness and an innate goodness that made her radiant inside and out. When it came to beauty, Emma was the real deal. Blair was an expertly wrapped but empty Christmas package by comparison. All glitter and no substance.

He thought of the easy way Emma had of drawing him into conversation and how comfortable she was to be around. He thought of her kiss and how perfectly she fit into his arms. He and Emma belonged together, and he wished to God it was her with him today, instead of Blair.

He drew in a breath and slowly released it. His own feelings aside, he wondered how Mick would handle seeing his mother.

"He might not be happy to see me at first," Blair said, as if hearing his thoughts.

"That's a possibility."

"I know I let him down, Shane, but I'm going to make up for that. Starting today." She lit a cigarette and blew a stream of smoke at the windshield. Her cell phone jingled and Shane's thoughts returned to Emma and the sweet smell of her hair. He wondered what she was doing at that very moment.

When they reached the hospital, he instructed Blair to wait in the corridor by the nurse's station. "Let me feel him out, see how he reacts to your being here. I'll come and get you as soon as I know he's all right with it."

She started to protest and he held up his hands. "Let's do it my way for once, alright?"

She rolled her eyes. "Fine."

"You'll wait right here until I call you?"

"Yes, Shane, I'll wait right here." With an exaggerated sigh, she grabbed a magazine from the table and flipped it open.

The activities room was more crowded than it had been the day before. Mick sat in the same chair by the window, but today he greeted Shane with a smile.

"Hey, Dad."

"Hey."

"We're scheduled for a counseling session this morning, did they tell you?"

"Yeah, I talked to your doctor first thing this morning."

"How's everything at the campground?"

Shane hesitated, gauging Mick's mood. "Everything's fine."

"How's Emma?"

"Emma's fine, too."

"Is she mad at me?"

"Why would she be mad at you?"

"For stealing her car."

"She's not mad at you, Mick. Nobody's mad at you."

Mick stretched his arms. "This place is so boring it almost makes school seem like a thrill park."

Shane chuckled. "Try and remember that next week, will you?"

They spent the next few moments talking about the television program Mick had watched the night before. Completely out of the blue, he said, "Hey Dad, remember when we used to go fishing up at Tupper Lake?"

The question caught Shane off guard. He thought of the handful of weekends he'd taken Mick to the fishing retreat for some father-son bonding when Mick was small. They'd spent the days fishing, and the nights sitting around a campfire, telling stories and toasting marshmallows. Shane had intended for it to be a yearly ritual but when he took over the campground the father-son weekends got lost in the shuffle like so many of his good intentions. The last time they'd gone was nearly a decade ago and he was surprised Mick even remembered it.

"Sure, I remember."

"Do you think we could do that again some time?"

"I'd like that."

"So would I."

"What made you think of that, Mick?"

"I dunno. Last night in our group session the counselor told us to think of our happiest memory. Somehow those weekends at Tupper Lake came into my—" He broke off in mid-sentence as his gaze shot to the door, and then returned to Shane in anger. "What's she doing here?"

Before he could formulate an answer, Blair hurried across the room and threw herself at Mick. She grasped him around the neck, sobbing. "My baby! Mickey, what's happened to you?"

Every person in the room turned to stare and Shane felt his blood begin to boil. Why did Blair always have to be so theatrical? Why did she always have to be the star of the show?

"I'm fine, Mom," Mick said, peeling her arms from around him.

"Are you really, Mickey? I've been so worried." She dabbed her eyes with a Kleenex. "Stand up and give Mom a hug."

Mick complied, looking more than a little uncomfortable. Watching her at that moment, Shane's eyes were opened and he could see with crystal clarity the things he hadn't been able to see at eighteen, at twenty-five, or even at thirty. He could see Blair for the spoiled, self-absorbed person she was and always had been. For the first time, he was glad she came back. Now there would be nothing left unresolved, no niggling doubt in his mind about what might have been. For now and forever, that chapter of his life was closed. It was time to move on. It was time to start writing the rest of his life story.

Chapter Fourteen

As soon as Shane and Blair left the campground Emma and Dusty rolled up their sleeves and went to work, starting with the flower beds at the campground's entrance. She'd been full of good intentions, but her confidence wavered as she stared at the profusion of flowers, feeling completely overwhelmed.

"We took notes at the park, but now I can't remember what the plan was," she confessed.

"Let's put the geraniums out front," Dusty suggested. "They'll like the shade."

"Works for me." She grabbed a flat of red geraniums, mixing in white petunias and a sprinkling of miniature delphinium in a vibrant shade of blue. Carrying them to the bed, she knelt and removed them from their pots as Dusty worked a bag of organic topsoil into the bed. Though she'd never considered herself much of a gardener, she found the act of planting flowers satisfied something basic deep inside her soul. She hummed as she worked, enjoying the sun on her back and the feel of the dark, rich soil beneath her hands.

"Don't go too deep with those, Emma," Dusty warned. "Just cover the roots."

Removing the geranium, she carefully replaced some of the soil before setting it back in the hole. She couldn't help smiling at the change the simple act of flower planting seemed to have wrought in Dusty, as well. Gone was the self-conscious, stammering man who met her on the porch that morning. The man who worked beside her was knowledgeable and self assured.

"You seem to know a lot about gardening," she commented.

Dusty shrugged and turned a shovelful of soil. "I used to have a big old barn of a house on the other side of the lake. My wife and I always planned to put on a porch and vinyl siding. We couldn't ever seem to afford the home improvements we wanted, so we made up for it by having the prettiest yard on the block."

Emma dug a shallow hole with her trowel and set in a geranium. "I wish I could have seen them. I'll bet they were lovely."

"That they were." Dusty smiled at some far away memory. "Soon as our daughter was old enough to hold a shovel I dug up a plot just for her. Her own little garden. I spent hours looking through seed catalogues with her, but she never wanted to plant anything but sunflowers."

"Emma shaded her eyes with her hand and looked up at Dusty. "What was her name?"

"Chelsea."

He turned back to his work, his smile all at once chased away by sadness. Respecting the gravity of the moment, Emma fell silent.

"I heard the things you told Mick that night," Dusty said after awhile. "We're the same in that way, you and me. I know what it is to lose someone, to feel like you can't go on, not for one more day, one more hour."

"You can't go forward and you can't go back," she said quietly.

"You're in a good place here, Emma. Shane's a good man. He'll treat you right."

Emma felt her face grow hot and quickly turned back to her work, sensing Dusty wasn't speaking of Shane as just her employer.

•

"I would have thought he'd have been at least a little bit happy to see me." Blair speared a black olive with her fork, popped it into her mouth, and chewed angrily. "I am his mother, after all."

"He warmed up after awhile," Shane said, barely able to mask his irritation. "You've got to admit it was quite a shock to him. Especially the way you went bursting in there. I thought I asked you to wait."

"I didn't appreciate being left in the hallway like some kind of naughty servant," she shot back. "I had every bit as much right to see him as you."

Technically she was wrong. When she left, Blair had made Shane Mick's sole guardian, but at the moment he was too fatigued to argue the point. He gazed out the oversized window of the diner into the late afternoon sunlight. All things considered, the counseling session had gone better than he'd hoped. And if Shane was less than ecstatic at his ex-wife's sudden invasion back into his life, Mick was obviously pleased that Blair was there. Shane had seen it just beneath his son's veneer of angry indifference. He only hoped Blair wouldn't start making empty promises. She'd seen for herself that Mick was alright, and he hoped she wouldn't hang around for too much longer.

Once again displaying an uncanny ability to read his mind, she said, "He needs me. I thought being a teenager he'd be all right if I left, but obviously he isn't. I'm going to stay awhile. Maybe permanently."

Shane felt as if he'd been hit with a hammer. The air in the diner was suddenly stifling hot and he felt like he was suffocating. He gaped at her, unable to make words form from the thoughts that tumbled around inside his head.

"You don't have to look so grumpy."

"You couldn't stand to be here," he said acidly. "You felt like the walls were closing in on you—those were your exact words. And now you want to come back?"

"Things change. The grass isn't always greener elsewhere. Isn't that what they say?"

"You picked a hell of a time to find that out," he said, glaring at her.

"Why? Because of your new girlfriend?"

"This has nothing to do with Emma!" He said it louder than he intended. Several people turned from their meals and craned their necks in curiosity.

"Correction. This has nothing to do with you and me, Shane, so let's get that straight right now." She speared another olive. "I know the situation is awkward, but I'd hoped we could at least be civil to one another for Mick's sake."

Shane fought to keep his temper in check. Why did this woman always seem to bring out the beast in him?

"Let's not make any major decisions right now, okay?"

She popped a forkful of salad into her mouth and chased it with a swallow of water. "I called my boss this morning and arranged a month's leave of absence."

"Without talking to me first?"

"Yep."

Shane pushed away his plate, his appetite soundly spoiled. A month would seem like an eternity. He hoped to God he and Blair could make it that long without killing one another.

•

That evening Emma stood back to admire her handiwork. She smiled with satisfaction at the flowers, cheerful and welcoming in their beds. It was her way of welcoming Mick home, and she hoped that in some small way he would take notice and be pleased.

She heard the rumble of exhaust moments before Shane's truck pulled into the lot. The passenger's side door opened and Blair climbed out, the storm clouds on her face soundly chasing away Emma's smile.

Brushing past Emma, she stormed toward the cabin, stopping to survey the flower beds by the front walkway. "Red, white and blue. How patriotic," she said, her voice dripping with sarcasm.

Shane climbed from the truck, looking every bit as stormy as his ex-wife. His expression softened as it came to rest on Emma.

"You've been busy today," he said. "This looks fantastic."

"Dusty and I worked on it for most of the day. We couldn't f-find your sketches, but even so, I think it turned out pretty good."

Blair frowned. "I don't remember ever doing the front in red, white and blue. We've always gone with warm, vibrant colors."

"Change can be good," Shane said, glowering at her.

"Or not," she said, returning his icy stare. "I'm going to take a shower."

Emma watched as she stalked toward the cabin. When the door slammed shut behind her, she turned back to Shane. "How did it go today?"

"There were a few bumpy spots to say the least. But the session went pretty well. At least Mick didn't lock himself in his room like I thought he would. Is there anything going on here that I need to know about?"

"Three campers checked in. I put them in area four. And one of the pipes in the bath house sprung a leak. Dusty's down there now."

He sighed. "I should probably go down and give him a hand." Their eyes met. Emma sensed there was more he wanted to say and she wasn't at all sure she was ready to hear it.

"I should go and get cleaned up. I think I've got more dirt on me than in the flower beds. I'll see you tomorrow," she said, hurrying away.

"Emma?" His voice cut through her like a blade. Steeling herself, she turned back.

"Can I come by and see you later?"

His expression was grave and Emma felt her heart constrict.

"If you w-want to."

"It'll probably be an hour or so, depending on how bad the leak is."

Walking back to her cottage, Emma felt her heart trip inside of her and she knew with a sick certainty it was about to get broken again.

Thirty minutes later she stepped out of the shower, wrapped herself in her robe, and vigorously toweled her hair dry before heading to the kitchen. She halved a bagel and was searching in the back of the fridge for a stick of butter when she heard a sharp rapping at her front door. Alarmed, she glanced at the clock. He couldn't be here already, could he? Clutching her robe close around her, she opened the door. Blair stood on the other side.

"Can I talk to you for a minute?"

Too stunned to do anything else, Emma stepped aside to let her enter.

Blair's ocean blue eyes swept across the room before coming to rest on Emma. "Listen, I wanted to say thanks. I understand you really went the extra mile to help Mick out the other night."

The words caught Emma off guard, rendering her speechless.

"I wanted you to know how much I appreciate it, that's all."

"It was the l-least I could do," she said, finding her voice. "He's a great kid."

"Yes, he is." She paused. "Look, I don't know what Shane's told you about me, but just remember, there are two sides to every story."

"Whatever happened b-between you and Shane is none of my business."

The words seemed to please her. "I know Mick's angry with me for leaving, but I had my reasons. I think with time we can work through it. Whether he wants to admit it or not, he still needs his mother."

"Of course he does."

"I guess you know that he's coming home tomorrow. I'm hoping we can start being a family again."

Emma felt a pang of sadness and did her best to keep it from her face.

"I don't know what's between you and Shane and I'm not asking. He's free to do as he wants. All I ask is that you try and think of what's in Mick's best interests."

"Meaning?"

"Meaning we all have to put our own preferences aside right now and try to get him through this. He doesn't need to be hurt any more than he already has been."

"I'd never do anything to hurt Mick."

"I'm counting on that, Emma."

She turned and walked from the cottage, leaving her words hanging over Emma like thick, dark clouds.

•

That night, Shane strode down the pathway to Emma's cottage, picking his way through the dark. The lamps he'd installed along the path had malfunctioned again. He'd have to add that to his ever growing list of things to take care of. He sighed, weary to the core of his being. It was nearly nine o'clock when he and Dusty finally finished up in the bath house. He'd returned to the cabin to shower and change and gotten tangled up in an argument with Blair. Now it was after ten. He hoped Emma hadn't given up on him and gone to bed.

Rounding a bend in the path, he saw the glow of lights behind her windows and relief pooled in his gut. He missed her so badly he was damned near suffering withdrawal symptoms. He climbed the stairs, taking a moment to rake his fingers through his hair in an effort to tidy it before knocking on the door. He heard the sound of footsteps approaching and then the door opened and Emma stood before him, looking soft and pretty in a rose-colored bath robe. He jammed his hands in his pockets, resisting the urge to pull her into his arms.

"I didn't think you were coming," she said.

"I'm sorry. I got held up." His gaze moved over her in a gentle caress. "Can I come in?"

After a moment's hesitation she stood aside to let him in. He stood in the living room, awkwardly shifting his weight and wondering at the guarded expression in her eyes. There were a hundred and one things he wanted to say to her, but all at once he wasn't sure she wanted to hear them.

"What time will Mick be home tomorrow?" she asked, breaking the silence.

"Early afternoon. The doctor wants to check him over one more time, make sure he's good to go."

"Are you scared?"

"A little. I mean, he seems okay, but I'm going to have to keep a close eye on him. At least for awhile. I'm hoping you, Dusty and Alex can help me out with that."

"Of course." She moved to the bank of windows and stood looking out at the lake. "Blair says she's going to stay."

It was a simple statement but Shane detected a subtle undercurrent of pain in her words and he again cursed his ex-wife's timing. "She'll be sleeping in the guest room."

"That's none of my business."

He took a step toward her. "Blair's being here doesn't change anything."

Her eyes met his briefly before falling away. "It changes everything."

Throwing caution to the winds, he took her in his arms. "It doesn't change the way I feel about you." She tried to move from his embrace and he held her tighter. "There's something happening between us, Emma. Don't tell me you don't feel it, too."

"L-let me go," she said firmly.

His arms released her, but his eyes refused to. "I never wanted her back here. I'm only letting her stay because I think she and Mick need to sort things out. I'm not going to let that interfere with us."

"There is no us, Shane."

Disappointment crashed through him. "Don't say that, Emma. I thought we were starting to—"

"I kn-know what you thought, but you were wrong." She took a breath. Slow down, Emma. Start again. "You're my boss. Nothing more. I already told you that."

"Is that really how you feel?"

She nodded.

Recovering from the blow, he steeled himself against his

disappointment. Shot down twice. What kind of a fool was he? Without another word, he turned and strode from the cottage, firmly closing the door on any foolish notions he'd harbored about love and happily ever after.

•

Emma wiped away a tear as she watched Shane's broad shoulders disappear down the path. Her heart ached inside of her, ached to call him back and tell him the truth. But loving him as she did, how could she stand in the way of his happiness? He was angry with Blair right now, but it was clear to Emma that Mick wasn't the only one with issues to sort through. The three of them had been a family once. If there was a chance they could be again, how could she be the one to destroy that chance? How could she selfishly sabotage the futures of the people she'd come to care about, to love? She couldn't and wouldn't.

All she could do is step aside and let nature take its course, no matter how much it hurt.

Chapter Fifteen

On Saturday night Shane sat on his porch drinking a bottle of beer and enjoying his first relaxing moments of the day. He watched the sun's slow setting over Shadow Lake and felt his stress begin to ease. Mick had been home for three days. Shane was doing his best to be positive, to try and smooth the wrinkles out of his son's first days home, but God knew Blair wasn't making it easy. In fact she was driving him damn near to the end of his rope. He drained his beer bottle and filled his lungs with the soft, perfume-scented air, willing his knotted muscles to relax.

How had he put up with her all those years?

Tying up the bathroom for hours on end and butting her cigarettes in the house plants, those were things he could have overlooked. What he couldn't live with was the way she constantly corrected and analyzed him, always making him feel that he didn't measure up to some secret set of standards. He'd been blessedly free of that for a year. Now he was back to working long hours just to avoid being home.

Thoughts of Emma invaded his mind. He'd been avoiding Emma, too, but for entirely different reasons. There had been a flame between them. For some unfathomable reason it had grown cold. Was it because of Blair, or because of him? He felt like a failure and he wasn't even sure what he'd done wrong. Why was it that when it came to women he always seemed to come out on the losing end?

Without warning the door opened and Blair's voice scattered the quiet. "How come you're sitting out here all alone?"

"Just trying to enjoy the quiet."

"Want some company?" Not waiting for an answer, she crept behind him and began to knead his shoulders. "You've been working too hard. Your muscles are all knotted. "

"The campground isn't going to run itself," he said testily.

"Then why don't you let me help? I used to be pretty efficient, if I remember correctly."

"It's not your responsibility any more, Blair."

"We used to make a pretty good team," she said, applying deep pressure to his shoulders. "Why don't we try again?"

He turned and stared at her in amazement. "Try what?"

"Us."

He could see by her expression that she was dead serious. If he hadn't been sitting Shane would have fallen over. "That's not an option."

"Of course it's an option. We've got history together, a child—"

"You're Mick's mother and nothing is going to change that. But you're not my wife any more and you never will be again."

"I'm not saying we have to remarry. At least not right now. But we used to be pretty good together." She brought her lips to his ear, whispering, "Why don't you let me sleep in your room with you tonight. We'll give it a trial run."

He jerked away as if she'd thrown battery acid on him. "Have you lost your mind?"

Her lips pursed in an angry pout. "Is it because of her?"

"No, it is not because of Emma! It's because of you, Blair, don't you get that? It's over between us, and that was your decision, not mine."

He stood and strode into the house, slamming the door behind him. In his room, he stretched out on his bed and punched his pillow. A trial run. How did she have the nerve to even suggest such a thing? How could she play with him like a child who discards a toy, leaves it mangled and broken, only to decide she wants it back again? How, in just a few short days, had she managed to turn his entire life inside out?

He drew a deep, calming breath. He and Mick would be going to Tupper Lake in the morning to spend some much needed time away. With any luck a few days and a few hours distance would help him sort out the mess his life had become.

•

On Sunday morning Emma watched from the window as Shane and Mick packed their gear into the back of the truck. Mick walked with a noticeably lighter step that morning, and she knew how much the outing meant to him. He'd stopped by her cottage earlier to say goodbye and to pick up the care package she'd prepared for him and Shane.

Shane ...

He was back to giving her the silent treatment and she couldn't say she blamed him. She watched until they drove away, and then refocused her thoughts on the morning ahead. Walking to the back of the store, she put the coffee pots to work for the permanents who would soon start arriving for their Sunday morning papers and chatter.

Hearing a truck pull into the alley, she smiled, knowing it would be Sammy with the morning's delivery of baked goods. A retired high school history teacher, Sammy Delaney claimed he delivered for The Betty Kaye Bake Shoppe to make ends meet, but Emma suspected it was more out of a need to socialize than anything else. The elderly man was always ready with a smile and an interesting bit of trivia and she'd come to look forward to his visits. He was a gentleman and a scholar, and Emma thought, not for the first time, he was the grandfather she would have liked to have had.

"Morning, Sammy," she greeted him as he walked in.

"Hello, Emma. Beautiful morning out there, isn't it?"

"It sure is." He carried a tray of donuts, and Emma took it from his hands. "Oh, those look heavenly."

"Be sure to save one out for yourself." He added with a wink, "I had Betty put in an extra one of those peanut covered ones you like."

"You're the best," she said, depositing the tray on the counter. "Would you like a cup of coffee?"

"Maybe just half a cup for the road."

Emma poured him a cup and they chatted for a moment about the mild weather until Sammy's watch beeped.

"Uh-oh. Time's up," Emma said with a grin.

"You know me. I like to stay on schedule."

She followed him to the porch and bent to retrieve the stack of morning newspapers. The front door of the cabin opened and Blair stepped out onto the porch wearing an oversized bath robe that Emma assumed was Shane's. Noticing Emma there, she waved. Emma waved back, astonished to see that Blair was actually smiling at her.

Sammy's expression became uncharacteristically dark. "She's back, is she?"

"Yes, home for a visit."

Sammy grunted and Emma shot him a questioning glance.

"I've had many a run in with that one. As mean-spirited a woman as they come."

Before Emma could comment, Sammy's smile reappeared. "Have yourself a lovely day, Emma. I'll see you tomorrow morning."

"Ten o'clock sharp," Emma said, grinning again.

Returning back inside, Emma separated the newspapers, setting aside the ones reserved by the permanents and putting the rest in a rack beside the front counter. She'd just placed the money in the cash register for the day when the front door opened and Blair swept inside.

"Good morning, Emma," she said brightly.

"Good morning, Blair."

"I waited to come over until you got rid of that old fool. Is that coffee I smell?"

"Uh-huh."

"You're an absolute angel," she said, sauntering to the back of the store. "We ran out this morning. I wouldn't have come out of the house looking such a mess, but I can't seem to wake up without it."

As she poured a generous cup, Emma's gaze swept over her. Aside from being dressed in a ratty old robe, Blair was stunning, her hair and makeup salon perfect. Emma busied herself with yesterday's receipts, hoping Blair would take her coffee and leave, but for some reason she lingered.

"I really like the way you've rearranged the store, Emma. It's much more efficient this way."

"Thanks."

"I hope you don't mind if I stay for a minute or two. It's so quiet in the house this morning with both of them gone."

"I can imagine."

"They wanted me to go along but I told them they needed to get the male bonding thing going." She chuckled. "Between you and me, I'm not much for roughing it."

Of that Emma had no doubt. An uncomfortable silence

enveloped them and she searched her mind for something to talk about, coming up empty.

"Do I look as messy as I feel?" Blair asked.

"I think you look lovely."

"I can't imagine that, after last night." She chuckled again. "I'd nearly forgotten how much stamina Shane's got." Seeing Emma's stricken look, she added, "Oops. Guess that was a little too much information, huh?"

Emma gripped the edge of the counter, feeling like she'd be sick.

"I don't mind telling you, I feel positively giddy. Just like a teenager with her first boyfriend. Of course, Shane was my first boyfriend. We have so much history together. I never really realized how big a part of my life he was until I left."

Despite her rolling stomach, Emma forced a smile.

"Anyway, I want you to know how much I appreciate that you were willing to get out of the way."

"Excuse me?"

"You know, bow out gracefully. "

"Don't m-mention it."

"Well, I'd better scoot before someone comes in and sees me dressed like this. I'll come over for lunch later, we'll talk. Goodness, I hardly know anything about you at all."

Emma watched as Blair breezed from the store, her eyes stinging with tears. She'd done the right thing, but knowing that didn't make it hurt any less. What hurt the most was how quickly Shane had changed his mind. She'd honestly thought he cared for her, even dared to hope that he truly did love her. Why was it that love and pain always seemed to go hand in hand?

The door opened again and Dusty walked in. "Emma, do you know where the blasted weed whacker is? I can't find it any—" Seeing her expression, he stopped in mid-sentence. "Are you all right?"

"I'm fine," she said, forcing another smile.

His eyes narrowed in anger. "I saw her leaving just now. Did she say something to upset you?"

"No. She was very p-polite. Friendly, even."

He snorted. "That's not like her. Wonder what she wants?"

"Dusty, do you know of any other campgrounds in the area?"

"Campgrounds?" He scratched his chin. "Well, let me think. There's Daybrook over in Sparta, but it's not near as nice a place as this. Why do you ask?"

"I'm th-thinking of looking for new job."

"She did upset you."

"It isn't just B-blair. I'm feeling it would be best all the way around if I m-moved on." She couldn't bear to say the words out loud or even think them, but how could she stay, feeling the way she did?

"You don't really want to go, do you Emma? She'll get tired of whatever game it is she's playing and then she'll leave. Things will get better again."

"I don't think so."

"Promise me you won't make any decisions until you've talked to Shane, will you do that?"

"Okay."

"I've got to get at those weeds over in area four. If I can find the weed-whacker."

"I saw it propped up behind the old shed yesterday, when I was l-looking for a flower pot. It's behind the wheelbarrow."

"You see, that's why we need you around here. You keep us straight."

Despite Dusty's reassurance, Emma knew the campground wasn't big enough for both her and Blair. And it didn't look as though Blair was leaving any time soon.

When the door closed behind Dusty she poured a cup of coffee and opened the newspaper. Flipping to the Classifieds section, she skimmed through the ads. A hopeless feeling overtook her as she read through the listings. It was the same old batch of jobs she didn't come close to being qualified for. Nurses. Waitresses. School teachers. Sighing, she turned the page. An advertisement in bold blue print jumped out at her:

> *Get paid to live in a resort! Beautiful health spa and resort in the foothills is seeking qualified individuals for immediate employment. All positions needed. Housekeeping. Cooks. Wait staff. Great Pay. Free housing. Call toll-free 24/7.*

Feeling a flutter of hope, she re-read the ad. Surely she could clean motel rooms, couldn't she? The door opened again and Bess Sanderson, Emma's favorite of the permanents, strode in. "Morning, Emma. Got any fresh donuts today?"

"Sammy dropped them off a half hour ago," Emma told her. "I put one of the chocolate ones away for you."

"That's my girl."

Sliding the paper under the counter, Emma went to wait on her.

Chapter Sixteen

Shane watched the campfire die down to glowing embers, enjoying the quiet and the unaccustomed amity between himself and his son. All in all it had been one of the nicest days he could remember.

The weather had co-operated beautifully, with a warm breeze whispering across the lake beneath a perfect sailor blue sky. Setting out early, he and Mick found a perfect sink hole. They spent the better part of the day casting their lines into the clear blue lake, no clogged drains or ex-wives to worry about, just him and Mick and their fishing poles. They'd caught four good-sized bass, not at all shabby for a pair of beginners.

That evening when the sun went down they sat around the campfire outside their tent, full of the buttery sweet cornbread Emma had sent along for the trip and batter fried fish and thermoses of strong, hot coffee. They'd somehow reached a place of easy camaraderie and Shane wished he'd never discontinued the outings. For a few days, in this magical place, he and Mick could be equals—a pair of novice fishermen enjoying the great outdoors.

"Think I should put another log on the fire?" Mick asked, breaking into his thoughts.

"That might not be a bad idea. If I remember right it can get pretty chilly up here at night."

Mick threw another log on the fire, prodded it to flames with a stick, and then sat back down. Shane watched with a twinge of disappointment as he fished his cell phone out of his pocket and turned it on. After a few seconds he flipped it closed again. "Must be we're too far out to get a signal."

"Important business?" Shane asked.

"I promised Mom I'd call her tonight."

"Oh." Shane felt a stab of regret. He didn't want Blair's presence to intrude on the so-far perfect outing in even so small a way. But that was selfish and he knew it. "Take the truck to town if you want. You could call your mother from there."

Mick shrugged. "She's probably forgotten she even asked me to call."

Silence fell and Shane listened to the eerie sound of an owl hooting in a far off tree. He'd recovered a lot of ground with Mick that day, but hadn't been able to find a way to broach the subject that weighed heavily on his mind. Judging the moment to be right, he said, "She's probably not going to stay very long, Mick."

"I know."

"You do?"

"Some guy's been texting her. He's pretty hot for her to get back home."

The news shouldn't have surprised him, but somehow it did. "How do you know that?"

"She left her cell phone in the bathroom the other day. I read her messages."

"I see."

"I didn't know if I should tell you or not."

"It's none of my concern what she does."

"I didn't want you to be disappointed. But better now than later, I guess."

"What makes you think I'd be disappointed?"

"Because I know you were hoping to get back together with Mom."

"Is that what you thought?"

"Well, you called her and asked her to come home, didn't you?"

Shane nearly choked on his surprise. "Did she tell you that?"

"Yeah."

"She came back here for you, Mick. Not for me."

Mick poked at the ground with a stick. "You don't want to get back together with her, then?"

He pushed out a breath, not wanting to disappoint Mick, but as his son so sagely pointed out, better now than later. "No, I don't."

"That's a relief."

"It is?"

He shrugged. "She's my mom and I love her, but I don't want her to stay. She makes everything too stressful."

Relief washed over Shane in waves. "Have you told her that?"

"I don't want to hurt her." His voice took on an edge. "Even though she has no problem hurting us."

"I guess we're all going to have to sit down and talk some things over when we get home."

Mick whistled through his teeth. "She'll probably, like, go all ballistic on us."

Despite himself, Shane grinned. "Probably."

They sank into silence, the quiet broken only by the crackling fire and the owl's relentless cries.

"Dad?"

"Yeah?"

"Do you want to go into town anyway?"

"What did you have in mind?"

"I saw a Dairy Queen on our way in. We could get a couple of blizzards."

"Let's do it."

As he and Mick kicked dirt onto the campfire, Shane felt lighter than air. He wasn't sure exactly what Blair's game was, but he was glad that Mick didn't want to play any more than he did. He'd break the news to her as soon as he arrived home. After that he'd tell Emma exactly how he felt with no more dancing around the subject. And then, hopefully, they could all move on.

Chapter Seventeen

"Emma, be a sweetie and grab me a bottle of flavored water from the fridge." Blair sat at the desk in the office, painting her fingernails and flipping through a fashion magazine. "Kiwi strawberry would be great if we have any left."

"Kiwi strawberry it is," Emma said, holding her temper in check. Lord knew it wasn't easy. In three days' time Blair had set herself up as mistress of the campground. With Shane away she was as officious as a queen bee in a hive, making outrageous demands on them all and Emma was getting tired of it. Whereas Shane treated his employees with fairness and respect, Blair treated them like her personal servants.

In the kitchen she opened the fridge and rummaged for a bottle of flavored water, still fuming as she thought how Blair had assigned Alex the task of washing and waxing her car, while Dusty was commissioned to wash all of the windows in the cabin, inside and out. She'd had Emma take her clothes to the dry cleaner's, only to ask her to run back to town an hour later when she ran out of her favorite hair gel. Earlier that morning she'd given Emma a bleach stick and asked her to remove the stains from her white sandals. Emma'd spent three long days biting her tongue but her patience was stretched to its limit.

Returning to the office, she saw that Blair was on the phone.

"All right, darling. I can't wait to see you. Give Mick a hug for me."

Disconnecting the call, she gave Emma a bright smile. "I can't imagine I went a whole year without seeing Mick and Shane. They've only been gone three days and I'm counting the moments until Friday when they come back home."

Setting the water on the desk, Emma moved to the file cabinet and opened the drawer. Stowing the bank bag inside, she softly closed it again. "It sounds like they're having a fabulous time, though."

Blair's expression betrayed surprise. "You've talked to them?"

"I talked to Mick this morning."

"Did you?"

"Uh huh."

That morning Alex had misplaced the key to the golf cart and Emma'd called Mick on his cell phone to find out where he kept the spare. He'd chatted for a moment about the campground he and Shane were staying in and about the fish they'd caught. The conversation had been brief but she wasn't about to tell Blair that. The truth was she felt a secret sense of satisfaction in seeing the annoyance on Blair's face. As quickly as it appeared, though, Blair's dark expression vanished.

"Mick likes you, Emma, that's very obvious. I'm appreciative that you've been such a positive influence on him."

Sensing there was more, Emma waited.

"Lord, this isn't easy," Blair murmured. Turning her sky blue eyes on Emma, she said, "I think it would be best if you weren't here when they got home."

An icy fist closed around Emma's heart. "What?"

Blair removed an envelope from the drawer and slid it across the desk. "You know Shane and I have decided to try and make it work, to give our marriage another try, for Mick's sake. Frankly, I think Shane has feelings for you. I think it would be best to keep temptation out of reach, if you know what I mean."

Emma stared at her, momentarily unable to make sense of her words. "I'm being dis-dismissed?"

"There's the equivalent of a month's pay in here. It's your severance pay. You're being given the chance to start over again, somewhere else," she said, emphasizing the last words. "Please don't take it personally, Emma. We both know this is what's best for everyone."

Emma held back her tears until she was safely inside her cottage. There was no way she was going to let Blair see her cry. When she finally let them come, her tears fell like a waterfall. The chance to start over again, Blair had said. Since Beck's death, she'd done nothing but start over—again and again and again. She was tired of recreating herself, tired of moving on. Glancing around the cottage, her gaze lingered on the cozy kitchen, the fireplace, the lake behind the bank of windows. She thought with sadness of the night Shane had brought her here. To think that she'd have to leave it all behind—leave Shane behind—broke her heart. She'd foolishly allowed herself to believe things would be different this time.

"Th-that's what you get for dreaming, Emma," she told herself.

Now she was homeless, jobless, loveless and damned near penniless. She was right back where she started.

She'd read the resort's ad a dozen times that week, and as many times had dialed the number, hanging up before the call rang through. Pulling it out of the wastebasket, she read it again. She'd drawn on an inner wellspring of strength when she'd applied for the job at Shadow Lake. She would have to draw on that strength again now that it was time to leave. Picking up the phone, she dialed the number listed in the classified ad.

This time she waited for an answer.

Chapter Eighteen

On Friday morning Shane drove away from Tupper Lake Resort feeling more relaxed than he had in months. He was also more determined. He and Mick had worked through some of their issues. Now it was time to take care of business at home—starting with Emma. This time he would not be ignored. He would not be shoved aside. She cared for him as much as he cared for her, and it was time they both admitted it.

Three hours later when he pulled into the lot at Shadow Lake, it took every ounce of self restraint he possessed not to rush into the store and confront her then and there. As he unloaded the camping gear from the back of the truck he couldn't keep his eyes from wandering to the store again and again. He'd been cold to her before he left, but even so, he'd thought she'd come out to welcome them home. When at last the door opened, he glanced up in anticipation, but it wasn't Emma who appeared. It was Blair.

She strode across the lot wearing a wide smile. Reaching the truck, she gathered Mick up in a hug. "I'm so glad you're home, Mickey. How was your trip?"

"It was awesome," Mick said, disentangling himself from her embrace. "Except I don't want to eat any more fish for at least a year."

She laughed, her eyes sliding to Shane. "How about you? Have a good time?"

"Like Mick said, it was awesome," he said, his gaze traveling back to the store.

"She's not here, Shane," Blair said.

She'd seen his thoughts plainly and he didn't bother denying them. "Where is she?"

"Well, I'm not really sure. She left here two days ago without saying anything to anyone. I would have thought she'd at least ..."

Shane couldn't hear the rest of her words for the alarm bells that were shrieking inside his head. "Why would she leave?"

"I don't know," Blair said with a shrug. "I guess she got a better offer."

He hurried toward the store, wanting, needing to see for himself. Blair followed close at his heels. "You don't need her anyway. I'm perfectly capable of running the store. I did it for years, after all."

Ignoring her, he pushed the door open and stepped inside. Quick glances left and right confirmed that the store was empty.

"I told you she wasn't here," Blair said testily, arms crossed in front of her chest.

He glared at her. "I don't suppose you had anything to do with her leaving?"

"Why on earth would you think that?"

"Call it a hunch."

Her tone softened. "I'll be honest, she did tell me she was quitting, and I didn't try very hard to stop her. She wasn't all that that capable. The poor thing was afraid of her own shadow. We make a much better team, you and me."

"We're not a team any more, Blair. When are you going to get that through your head?"

"We'll have to be a team now, won't we? It looks like you need me whether you want to admit it or not."

"I need you about as bad as I need a tax audit," he raged. "I could take out an ad and have someone new in here tomorrow."

"And you'd have to spend the rest of the summer training them."

"That's a sacrifice I'm willing to make."

"I should have known better than to expect a little bit of gratitude."

He stared at her, incredulous. "For what?"

"For helping you run this dump. For coming back at all. It's not like I wanted to, you know. I came to help Mick. I'm only staying for his sake."

"Mick doesn't want you here any more than I do."

"You don't know what you're talking about. Honestly, Shane, how much rejection am I supposed to take from the two of you?"

"Sweetheart, you walked out of here free and easy a year ago and never even looked back, so don't talk to me about rejection! And don't feel you have to stay here now. Mick and I will be fine, so you can pack your bags and go back to where you came from."

"There's nothing I'd like more, believe me," she shouted.

"Then why don't you go?"

"Because I have nothing to go back to."

"What about your job?"

"That didn't work out. I lost that job a month ago. I'm sure you'll be delighted to know that I'm flat broke."

"What about the divorce settlement? You couldn't possibly have gone through all that money in a year."

"Every penny."

"So that's what it all comes down to, huh? From the start this whole thing has been about money?"

"Isn't everything?"

They glared at each other for a long moment, until without warning, Mick's voice broke the silence. "Mom, I'll give you the money if you'll just go."

Blair's expression crumbled to despair as the anger drained from her eyes. "Mick, honey I didn't mean that like it sounded."

Mick shrugged, his eyes riveted to the floor.

She took a tentative step toward him. "I care about you, Mick. I've just never been good at showing it, have I? I've never been very good at being a mother."

Shane couldn't bear the pain in Mick's eyes. An instinct stronger than any he'd ever known overcame him—the need to protect his son. "Blair, I think maybe you should—"

"Dad? Do you mind if I talk to Mom alone for awhile?"

His gaze moved from Mick to Blair and back again. "If that's what you want."

"Why don't the two of us go back up to the house where we can talk in private?" Blair said, already leading Mick away.

"Fine, then. I'll stay here and close up the store," Shane said, but they were already gone. He watched the door long after it closed behind them, resisting the urge to follow. Wasn't that one of Mick's biggest complaints, that his father treated him like a child? He sighed. Somehow his subconscious mind held Mick in place as that little boy lost at the zoo. In reality Mick was becoming a man before his eyes, a man who was able to think and speak for himself.

A man who no longer needed his father's protection.

A feeling of loneliness overcame him, along with an almost insatiable desire to be needed. Time was moving on. His son was moving on without him. In a couple more years Mick would be out on his own. Fear caused Shane to break out in a sweat. He didn't want to end up alone, no one to share his life with. Dear God, he didn't want to end up alone.

"Emma," he whispered, "Where are you?"

An hour later he locked up the store and headed for the house. He stood in the doorway, watching as Mick and Blair sat in the living room looking through old photo albums.

"What's going on?" he asked.

"Just reminiscing." Blair patted the space beside her on the sofa. "Come and sit with us."

He sat down beside her, keeping his distance in more ways than one. The last thing he wanted was to pretend they'd been a happy family, to pretend the smiling photos were anything more than a fantasy, a handful of make-believe moments contrived for the eye of a camera. To his relief, Blair closed the album.

"Shane, I want to go to Vegas," she said.

"Vegas?"

"I want to go to school and learn how to deal cards. I need a few hundred dollars to get there, and another couple thousand to get started."

He sat in silence, waiting for the other shoe to drop.

"There's lots of money to be made," she said in a rush. "You could think of it as an investment. I'd pay you back with interest, any amount you say."

He'd had a similar conversation with her the years before. It was DisneyWorld then, but this time he felt no anger, no resentment or sadness. The only desire he felt was to be rid of her, once and for all.

"Alright."

Her face broke out in a smile. "You mean it?"

"Yes, I mean it. But this is the last time I'm going to bail you out."

She threw her arms around him. "I'm going to pay it back, Shane. Every penny."

Jumping up from the couch, she hugged Mick, babbling about

the strip, the lights and the excitement, and the heartbeat of Las Vegas. "It's going to be fantastic, Mick. And as soon as I get settled I'm going to send you a plane ticket to come and visit me. You'd like that, wouldn't you?"

As Mick's eyes met his, Shane saw in them not only sadness, but pity. "Sure, Mom. It'll be great."

•

The next morning Shane awoke early and headed to the kitchen to find Blair's suitcases packed and waiting by the door. She sat at the table, chattering to Mick.

"Heading out already?" Shane asked.

"As long as I'm going I thought I might as well get an early start," she said cheerfully. "Thanks again, Shane."

She swept Mick up in a hug and pressed a kiss against his cheek. "I'll call you as soon as I'm settled in."

"Okay, Mom."

Shane walked her to her car, threw her suitcases in the back, and watched her drive away with a sigh of relief. Mick stood beside him, watching as his mother drove out of his life for the second time.

"Are you alright, kid?" he asked.

Mick nodded.

"Feel like breakfast?"

"Omelets?"

"Perfect."

In the kitchen, Shane cracked a half-dozen eggs into a bowl while Mick shredded a brick of cheddar cheese. "If you don't mind my asking, what did you say to your mother last night?"

"Lots of things," Mick said with a shrug. "I told her I'm tired of the fighting. Tired of pretending everything is okay with us. Mostly, I just told her I want us all to move on and don't think we can do that together. I guess I gave her permission to leave."

Shane thought about that for a moment. "And now that she's gone do you feel like you can move on?"

"Yeah, I guess I do." He scooped the pile of shredded cheese onto a plate and carried it to the stove.

"Dad?"

"Yeah?"

"Where do you think Emma went?"

"I wish I knew."

•

After breakfast Shane walked across the lot and opened the store. The campground seemed gloomy that morning, deprived of the sunshine of Emma's smile. His glance moved to the back of the store, to the place where she should have been.

I'm going to find you, babe. I'm going to find you and I'm going to bring you back here where you belong. Back to me.

He'd just started up the coffee pots when the front door opened and Mick walked in, Dusty following. Shane did a double-take. Dusty stood straight and tall, almost the man he'd known what now seemed an entire lifetime ago.

"Dad," Mick said, excitement coloring his voice. "Dusty's got something to tell you."

Dusty cleared his throat. "It's none of my business, but I think I might know where Emma is."

Hope surged inside him. "Where?"

"I went to clean out her cottage yesterday and I found this." He handed Shane a torn out newspaper page and Shane's eye was drawn to the ad in bold ink at the bottom.

"Get paid to live in a resort." He read through the ad, and then walked to the phone. "We'll see about that."

Grabbing up the receiver, he dialed the number listed in the ad. After three rings a breathy female voice answered. "Good morning, Cedar Valley Resort."

"Good morning. I'm calling about an ad I saw in the newspaper. It says I can get paid to live in a resort. I'm hoping to find some work."

"Yes sir, what sort of work are you looking for?"

"I'm a handyman, of sorts. I can do grounds-keeping, small engine repair, building maintenance. Most anything, really."

"We conduct interviews seven days a week, sir. Come on out and see us. I'm sure we can find you something."

He grabbed a nearby sales pad and a pen and jotted down the address she gave him. "Thanks very much. I have a feeling you'll be seeing me soon."

He hung up the phone, meeting Mick and Dusty's hopeful stares. "It's a resort over near Silver Springs, about four hours from here."

"Go and get her, Shane," Dusty said. "I can look after things here."

Shane didn't need to hear any more. His mind was made up, had been made up from the moment he learned of Emma's departure.

"What do you think, Mick? Are you up for another road trip?"

Mick's face broke out in a grin, telling him all he needed to know.

Chapter Nineteen

Emma wheeled her utility cart to the supply closet for what seemed the hundredth time that day. She stopped to massage an aching knot of muscles in the small of her back before replenishing her supply of cleaning solutions, toiletries, and towels. She had sixteen more rooms to render sparkling clean before her shift ended at six o'clock. She hoped she had the stamina.

Wheeling the cart to the service elevator, she glanced out the window at a breathtaking view of the compound. The resort was everything the brochures promised and more. If you happened to be a guest.

The seventy-five acre complex offered five star hotels set on perfectly landscaped grounds and included amenities like massages and indoor hot springs. Top-notch restaurants served exotic foods on plates of the finest bone china. In the daytime guests could enjoy golfing, tennis, horseback riding and swimming, not to mention shopping of every kind. For nighttime entertainment there were dance halls, clubs and movie theaters. Cedar Valley Resort's paying customers would find the complex more than satisfactory. But its employees ...

The resort's female workers were housed in the old section of the complex, in a dungeon of a building called Esbonshade. The structure had been built shortly after the Second World War and had seen very few improvements since. Esbonshade sat tucked away in a little corner of the woods, far removed from the grand hotels, like a shirt-tail cousin to be kept out of sight. The rooms were dormitory style, each furnished with a lumpy cot and a chest of drawers, with a shared bathroom on each of Esbonshade's eleven floors. When Emma was lucky enough to get a crack at a shower, there was often no hot water. Her housemates were mostly young girls between semesters at college, for whom waiting tables and cleaning toilets was a stop off on the road to something better. Like everywhere else in her life, she felt like a square cog in the resort's continuously turning wheels.

Be that as it may, she was stuck there. She'd left Shane a check for the amount she still owed on the car repairs. After paying rent on a storage cubicle large enough to hold her few pieces of furniture and the cost of shoes and uniforms, she had precious little money left. She thought of Shadow Lake with a pang of sadness. She'd done the right thing by leaving. Love meant sometimes sacrificing for the one you loved. And if doing the right thing meant another dose of heartache, well, she was certainly no stranger to surviving a broken heart.

•

"Oh, sweet." Mick let out a low whistle as the truck entered the parking circle at Cedar Valley Resort, echoing Shane's thoughts. The place was swank, he'd give it that.

His glance swept over the extravagant hotels with their manicured lawns and picture perfect flower beds before moving beyond them to a horseshoe of cobbled streets lined with upscale specialty shops. Maybe Emma's decision to leave had nothing to do with Blair at all. Maybe the campground had simply been a stepping stone to something more grand. The thought was painful. No one deserved luxury more than Emma, still …

The spa was pretentious and overdone, whereas Emma was uncomplicated and down to earth. She didn't belong in a place like this and he wasn't leaving until he convinced her of that.

Walking up the stone path that led to the Welcome Center, he took a moment to appreciate the building's old world charm, the cascading fountains out front encircled by marble benches. The place oozed class. Stepping inside, he half expected to see Emma sitting at the front desk. Instead he saw a Barbie Doll come to life. The woman smiled brightly as he and Mick approached, shaking her mane of sun streaked curls.

"Welcome to Cedar Valley Resort," she said in a deep, throaty voice. "Do you have a reservation?"

"Actually, no," Shane said. "I'm trying to locate on of your employees. A lady named Emma Beckman."

Her lips turned down in a frown. "Sir, we have dozens of

employees. I'm afraid names mean nothing to me."

Shane reached in his pocket and pulled out a fifty-dollar bill. "I was hoping you could look in your files and see if she's listed."

"I'm sorry," she said, her voice dripping with mock sincerity. "But our personnel files are highly confidential. I just don't think I can help you."

"I wonder how much cash it would have taken," Mick grumbled as they stepped outside.

"It was worth a shot."

"This place is huge. We're never going to find her."

"Yes we are," Shane said. "Let's try looking in some of the gift shops."

The resort seemed to cater to its guests' every whim, with shops featuring shoes, designer clothing, jewelry, perfumes and gourmet coffees. There was even a store that sold nothing but chocolates, Shane noted in surprise. He started at one end of the street while Mick took the other. An hour later they met in the middle.

"Any luck?" Shane asked.

"No. But I got this cool necklace," Mick said, securing a beaded hemp choker around his neck.

"I think we've about covered all of the shops. Where to next?"

"How about some of the restaurants?"

"Do you think she could be waiting tables?"

"I don't know, but I'm starving."

The resort's largest hotel featured an upscale restaurant called The Blue Moon. Shane slid into a seat at a table near the back, feeling embarrassingly underdressed and infinitely thankful the establishment was nearly empty. He scanned the restaurant, hoping beyond hope for a glimpse of Emma.

A cute blonde who looked to be about Mick's age bounded over to their table, water pitcher in hand. "You two look hungry," she chirped. "Would you like to hear about our dinner specials?"

"We're just having dessert," Shane told her.

"Okay. Our house specials tonight are deep dish apple pie and frozen strawberry soufflé. But if you're feeling dangerous, we also have a triple fudge brownie supreme that's to die for."

"Sounds good. I'll have that," Shane said.

"Make it three," Mick chimed in.

The waitress gave him a smile. She hurried away, returning

moments later with three heaping plates smothered in chocolate and whipped cream.

"I wonder if you could tell me whether or not my sister is working tonight," Shane said, laying the fifty in the center of the table.

The girl's eyes flitted to the bill and then back to Shane's face and he watched her vacillate between greed and company loyalty.

"Who's your sister?" she asked, giving up the fight.

"Emma Beckman."

Her brow wrinkled. "I don't know of any Emma in this department."

"That's strange. I'm sure she told me she was working here."

"What's she look like?"

She's the most beautiful woman in the world, with eyes as gentle as a summer rain and hair the color of a perfect autumn day.

"She's around thirty, five-foot-four inches tall, reddish brown hair, and gray eyes. She talks with a bit of a stutter."

"Oh, her. Yeah, she lives on my floor at the dorm. I think she might be in the housekeeping department."

Shane glanced at his watch. "She's probably done working for the day, then."

"That all depends on her shift. We have nearly three thousand rooms at the resort. There are guests coming in at all hours, so the housekeeping staff works around the clock."

"Thanks for your help."

"No problem." She snapped up the fifty, shoved it in her uniform pocket, and scuttled away.

They finished their dessert quickly and headed back to the resort's main entrance, where a dozen walkways branched off in various directions. Shane stared, undaunted, at the main hotel, and then at the smaller hotels that lined the paths. He'd find her if it took all night. And when he found her, he'd do whatever it took to convince her. One thing was for certain. No way in hell he was leaving here without her.

"So where do we start?" Mick asked.

"At the beginning. Where else?"

They re-entered the largest hotel and painstakingly searched all twenty floors. Each time he caught sight of a utility cart or a maid's uniform Shane's heart leapt, only to plummet again when it wasn't

Emma. His disappointment only fueled his determination.

"One down, forty-nine to go," he told Mick, as they returned to the lobby. "We'll find her if it takes all night."

"Something I can help you fellows with?"

Shane turned to see a security guard seated at the front desk. His eyes flicked from the bank of surveillance cameras on the wall to the guard's suspicion-filled eyes.

"No, we're just ..." From there he drew a blank.

Just what? Just casing out the hotel, stalking one of your employees?

"We're supposed to be meeting my mom here for the weekend," Mick interjected, "but I'm thinking this isn't the right place. Is this the Duchess?"

"The Duchess is next door," the guard informed them, arms folded across his chest. "This is the Emerald."

"See, Dad? I told you this wasn't the right one," Mick said, sounding supremely irritated. Giving the guard a salute, he said, "Hey, thanks a lot for your help."

"My pleasure."

He steered Shane from the hotel with the guard staring after.

"Nice save," Shane said when the door closed behind them. "How did you happen to know the names of the hotels?"

"Believe me, Dad, you don't want to know."

"Yeah, actually I do."

Mick reached in his oversized pocket and pulled out a stack of porcelain coasters, the names of each of the spa's hotels embossed in gold in their centers. "I sort of borrowed these from the restaurant. I thought they'd look cool on the coffee table. Lucky thing for us I've got light fingers, huh?"

"We'll talk about it later."

As they entered the lobby of the Duchess, Shane noted that it, too, was equipped with a security guard and cameras.

"Maybe we should split up," Mick said. "That way we won't look so suspicious. I'll start with the bottom floor and you can take the top. We'll meet in the middle again."

The plan made sense and Shane headed for the elevator, hoping to God their luck would hold. Stepping off the elevator, he caught the faint, honeysuckle scent of Emma's perfume before he noticed a utility cart parked outside the third door on the left. Heart pounding, he headed toward it. Walking past the room, he paused to glance inside. His breath lodged in his chest when he saw Emma emptying a wastebasket. Creeping past her line of vision, he lifted his hand to knock on the door.

"Yes?"

He heard soft footsteps approaching the doorway and then they were face to face. She was lovelier than ever before and he devoured every inch of her with his eyes.

"Hello, Emma."

Disbelief registered on her face. "Shane? What are you d-doing here?"

"I was just about to ask you the same thing."

Her gaze fell away. "I'm working."

"Emptying wastebaskets, huh?"

"There are w-worse jobs."

"Like running my store?"

Squaring her shoulders, she looked him in the eye. "I was replaced."

"No you weren't. Not even close."

"It doesn't matter. You shouldn't have come here."

"But now that I have, I've got some questions to ask you. And I'd really like some answers."

"I'm n-not going to argue with you, Shane, so if that's why you came ..."

"I came to find out why you left so suddenly. Why you couldn't even give me the courtesy of two weeks' notice."

Her gaze crashed to the floor again. "I th-thought it would be best."

Despite his heroic effort to keep it level, his voice cracked. "Best for who?"

She stared at the floor, not answering.

"Emma, I've been going out of my mind, wondering, worrying about you."

"No need to worry. I'm fine." She pulled in a breath, clearly working to control her stutter. "I'm s-sorry I didn't wait for you to get back before I left. It's just that this was such a good opportunity, t-too good to pass up."

"I want you to come back to Shadow Lake with me. I'll double your pay, if that's what it takes."

"I can't."

"Sure you can," he said softly.

"It's not about money."

"What, then, Emma? What is it about?"

She didn't answer, but the pain he saw in her eyes said it all.

"I'll tell you what it's about for me, then. I want to walk with you on the beach. I want us to play Yahtzee together, and plant flowers and eat pizza. I want you in my heart, and in my house, and in my bed." He knew he was making himself utterly vulnerable, wide open for a world of hurting if she didn't feel the same way. Even so, he forced the last words past the lump that thickened in his throat. "Emma, I want to replace your wedding ring. If you'll have me."

She lifted glistening eyes to meet his. "But we barely know each other."

"I know it doesn't make sense." His gaze rested tenderly on her face. "I fell in love for the first time as a kid, and I thought I knew it all. This time around I'm man enough to admit I don't know a damned thing, except what I feel. I love you, Emma. I want to spend the rest of my life getting to know you better. Isn't that what forever's for?"

Tears streamed from her eyes. "What about Blair?"

"Blair's gone."

"What do you mean, she's gone? I thought—"

"Right now she's on her way to Las Vegas to learn how to deal cards, or so she says. I don't know. Frankly, I don't care."

"But I thought the three of you were going to try and be a f-family again."

Reaching out, he took her face in his hands and forced her to meet his eyes. "That was never going to happen whether you stayed or not. Too much has changed. I've changed."

"What about Mick?"

"Right now he's somewhere in this hotel looking for you, ready and willing to make you see reason if you won't listen to me." He grasped her hands. "We want you in our lives, Emma. Forever. You deserve to be happy and I'm going to spend the rest of my life making sure you are."

His words took hold somewhere deep inside, mending a part of her that she hadn't known, until that moment, was broken. She'd allowed herself to take responsibility for Beck's death, believing deep inside that she wasn't deserving of happiness. As Shane gathered her up in his arms, she felt the unmistakable healing power of love, and something else; something wonderful and fragile that in time would deepen and become something magnificent.

"No more excuses, Emma. You're coming home with me, and I won't take no for an answer."

"Then I won't say no," she said, smiling through her tears.

As his lips claimed hers, she gave in to the sheer pleasure of his kiss, knowing there would be no more resisting. Knowing beyond a shade of doubt that she was starting over for the last time in her life.

•

Driving up the winding road that led to Shadow Lake, Shane gripped her hand as if he'd never let go of it again. Emma's gaze wandered to the hillside, where the vibrant greens, golds and ambers of the coming summer were made soft in the twilight. Beyond the trees the lake sparkled beneath the setting sun. She watched, lost in the sheer wonder of the moment, memorizing every shade and nuance of nature, and the feel of Shane's hand in hers, and the indescribable joy that filled her heart to overflowing.

As the last of the daylight slipped away, she thought about Beck. About endings, and how they led to new beginnings. She considered each of the beautiful people whose lives now interlocked with her own.

Mick, tumultuous and tender, a boy with a heart of gold who would grow into a man of excellence. Dusty, who'd lost so much, and become so much more than he thought he could be. And Shane ... Her hero. Her friend.

Each of them had walked through the valley of heartache and come out on the other side. And though the shadows that lingered in all of their pasts would never disappear completely, in time they would fade, like darkness fades in the light of a glorious new day.

• • •

Heatherfield

M. JEAN PIKE

M. Jean Pike

Author of HEATHERFIELD

In the
Shadow
of the
Dragonfly

M. Jean Pike

Photo by Sharon Burr

Abandoned buildings. Restless spirits. Love that lasts
forever. These are a few of M. Jean Pike's favorite
things. A professional writer since 1996, Ms. Pike
combines a passion for romance with a keen interest in
the supernatural to bring readers unforgettable stories
of life, love and the inner workings of the human heart.
She writes from her home on a quiet country road in
upstate New York.

www.ingramcontent.com/pod-product-compliance
Lightning Source LLC
Chambersburg PA
CBHW051842170626
46807CB00003B/1310